# THE AMAZING ADVENTURES OF REX FORD & CLAY HORN

by
Kenneth Lee McGee

To My Wife and Family,
You Are Everything

This Book is dedicated to the Native Americans
Unjustly treated over the years

All spelling mistakes in the manuscript are
completely intentional
(Except for the ones I missed)

Cover photograph by
Rachel Lynette French

All characters in this book are pure fiction
and created in the mind of the author.
Any resemblance to real people is a coincidence.
That includes the good guys, the Native Americans
and all those yeller-bellied, scum-suckin',
no-good-fer-nuthin' outlaws.

I remember my grandfather watching
Westerns on TV as he lay on the couch
in the living room of the farmhouse.
He would never miss an episode of
*Gunsmoke, Wagon Train,*
or any of his other numerous favorites.
My favorite was *The Lone Ranger*.
I loved the action compacted into thirty minutes.


I wrote these stories to approximate the
movie serials from the 30s and 40s.
Each of these would end in a cliffhanger with the hero,
or the damsel in distress, in grave peril.
Those of you who are old enough to remember
a more innocent time, sit back, relax and follow me
back to those thrilling days of yesteryear.

# Table of Contents

# ESCAPE FROM RIM ROCK

## A Rex Ford & Clay Horn Adventure

# Chapter One

"Whoa! Whoa!" I shouted as I slid to a stop on Loco, my blue roan horse.

I peered over the edge of the three hundred foot chasm looking for a way down. I ducked my head as I heard another bullet whiz past my ear.

"I hate to say it, but we're gonna have to find a way down unless we wanna get shot."

I looked over my shoulder at the onrushing posse, now only a hundred yards away. I encouraged Loco to forget about his fear of heights, or was that my fear? A bullet hit the dirt three feet to my left, raising a puff of white dust.

"Let's go, Loco!" I waved my white Stetson and over the edge we jumped.

After fallin' and slidin' for fifty feet, we miraculously landed on a three-foot-wide ledge. Dirt and small rocks cascaded down on us. I urged Loco forward with a shout. He snorted, then zoomed ahead.

"This ain't 'xactly a warm welcome to Arizonie, Loco."

Three minutes later we reached the bottom after a treacherous descent. I looked up at the *posse* as they waited at the edge.

"We cain't stick around, Loco."

He flipped his mane in agreement. I pulled on the reins and turned him to the right since I heard the rattle of a Western Diamondback warmin' itself on a flat rock to my left. We took off through the sagebrush in the direction that led to the open end of the box canyon. I heard the boom of a rifle, but knew we were out of range.

After meandering through the dusty, rocky canyon for a half hour, I looked back. "I don't think they're gonna follow us down that slope. I reckon we've bought ourselves a couple of hours at least," I told Loco. "I shore would like to know why they were shootin' at us, but I wasn't about to let 'em catch us so I could ask 'em."

Loco turned his head and snorted as if he understood. I swallered some warm water from my dented canteen. "Maybe somethin' happened in Rim Rock and they thought we had summat to do with it. That's all I can figure." I guessed we were gittin' close to the town the feller we saw at the tradin' post told us about two days ago.

Later that night as I sat under a rock outcrop twenty miles away from the box canyon, without a campfire, eatin' the last of some prairie chicken I picked up the day before, I pondered the day's events.

"Loco, ain't neither of us ever been to Rim Rock afore. Why would they be shootin' at us? Don't make a lick of sense. I'm just plain ol' Rex Ford from Roarin' Plains, Texas. I ain't been in Arizonie Territory but two days. We ain't seen more'n three people and a few buzzards."

I caught a few hours sleep and opened my eyes to bright sunshine. "Loco, I'm ready to head out if you are."

Just then I heard a bullet ricochet off the flat boulder three feet from my head.

## Chapter Two

"Let me see those hands, cowboy!"

Even though I couldn't see a soul, I raised my hands above my head as I sat up. Three men walked out of the mist holding shotguns which just happened to be pointed right at me.

"Keep them hands right whar I can see 'um." A man with a tin badge shouted. "Keep him covered."

I couldn't recognize any of the men, but I had no doubt they were from the posse that had follered me'n Loco yesterday. They chased us for 'bout an hour as we was gittin' close to the town I could see off in the distance in a valley between two stretches of pine-covered hills.

"I wouldn't make any sudden moves if'n you want to live." The man with the badge advanced slowly. "My name is Sheriff Dean and I need to have a few words with you back in Rim Rock."

"Can I stand up, sheriff?"

He nodded his head and I noticed the two other men circling about. I was real careful to move as slow as black-strap molasses in January.

"I'm Rex Ford from Roarin' Plains, Texas. Loco and I ain't never been in Rim Rock."

"That's somethin' we'll figure out when we get thar. Now we can do this a couple ways. I can handcuff you and make you ride thataway, or I can be more civilized and let you ride without bein' cuffed. Course, if I's to do that and you make a run fer it, I'd have to plug you plum full of holes with my shotgun."

"I'd rather ride without bein' cuffed I reckon if'n I have a choice."

He motioned me over toward Loco. The other two men had their shotguns on me as I saddled up.

"It's all right, Loco. We're gonna go for a ride with these men." I figgered I could make a break for it somewheres along the trail if I needed. "Mind if I ask why y'all were chasin' me yesterday?"

"We was a-chasin' you cause you was a-runnin'."

"Seemed like the right thing to do at the time since you were slingin' lead at me'n Loco."

Sheriff Dean motioned for the other two men to gather up my saddlebags.

"You don't mind if my deputies have a look-see now, do ya?"

"I ain't got nothing to hide." I noticed a rattler slither under a pile of rocks next to the scraggly mesquite tree I had slept under.

They picked up my bags, turned them upside down and dumped the contents out. All I was carryin' twas a clean shirt, britches and a little grub.

"Here's a picture of him and some girl, Sheriff. There's some writin' on the back."

"What does it say, Deputy Bonney?" Sheriff Dean asked, as he laughed.

"Ah, come on. You know I cain't read a lick." Deputy Bonney held out the picture so I could see it, as if I had more than one picture. "What's the writin' say, boy?"

"That's the ownliest picture I got of me'n my little sister Clara. She jest turned fifteen. The words on the back say that she's gonna miss me cuz I'm headed to Californy. Could you put it back for me?" I asked politely.

The deputies looked at the sheriff for an answer. He scowled at me, kicked at a scorpion, then nodded his head. Deputy Bonney put my picture back, then backed up into a barrel cactus. The sheriff shook his head. "Yer a dern fool, Bonney. Yer dumber than the rocks that slid down the mesa walls."

We mounted up and slowly began to head toward Rim Rock, I assumed.

"This is gonna take all day, so you just relax and you might live long enough to see the town." Sheriff Dean made sure I was covered by a shotgun at all times, so there was no opportunity to make a break for freedom. Since the land flattened out, and there weren't but a few scattered trees and sagebrush, I had no place to take any cover if'n I did make a run fer it.

As soon as we arrived in Rim Rock, I saw the new wooden structure at the edge of town.

"We've been anxious to try out that thar new hangin' contraption." Deputy Bonney laughed.

I moved a finger under my collar and tried to loosen it up. I certainly didn't want to be the main guest at a necktie party. My eighteenth birthday was only a week away.

An angry mob advanced toward me and the sheriff.

"There he is! That's the guy that shot the preacher man."

# Chapter Three

"Are we gonna string him up, Sheriff?"

"Yeah, we need to make shore them new gallows work right."

I wondered if I'd even make it inside the jail as the unruly mob closed in.

"Now hold on thar, Mr. Lambert. There ain't gonna be no hangin' in my town until the judge says so," Sheriff Dean asserted.

"But that's the guy." Mr. Lambert pointed at me. "Look at his horse and hat."

I was beginning to git a picture of what had happened. Someone ridin' a blue roan and wearin' a white Stetson had shot and kilt the local preacher man. I looked at the mob of enraged townsfolk and saw five other white hats. The sheriff and his deputies stayed between me and the crowd as I dismounted.

"Just stay calm, Loco. We'll git this straightened out right away." Loco shook his mane and snorted in reply as I loosely hitched him to the railing.

Sheriff Dean controlled the angry mob long enough to git me inside. I looked at the thick adobe walls and the two winder-less cells with their iron bars. I let my eyes wander around the single room. I felt safe enough for the time bein'.

I heard a set of keys jingle as Sheriff Dean tossed them to Deputy Bonney.

"Lock him up and you'n Deputy Hardin stay here whilst I go see if'n I can pry Judge Newman away from the saloon." He hitched up his britches and walked out the door. "And keep the door locked until I git back." I heard him shout.

"Git yoreself in that cell afore I shoot you," Deputy Bonney encouraged me with a shove from the butt of his shotgun in my back. I figgered he was just dumb 'nuff to shoot hisself.

I walked through the cell door and listened to the shriek of the rusty hinges as it it clanged shut behind me. I turned and placed my hands on the bars.

"I'm innocent. I ain't the right man."

"Yeah, well, Rex Ford, if'n that's really yore name, that ain't up to me." Deputy Bonney locked the cell, dropped the keys on the edge of the wooden desk eight feet away, sat down and leaned back like he owned the jail hisself. He pulled a pouch of tobaccy from his shirt pocket and bit off a chaw from the plug.

Deputy Hardin stared out the dirty winder at the slowly dispersing men.

"I h-h-hope Sheriff don't take too long to sober up ol' Judge Newman. I don't want to h-h-have this prisoner in h-h-here any longer than we h-h-hasta."

I didn't feel reassured in the least. I surveyed the jail. The back door looked pretty solid. I counted three shotguns leanin' against the far wall under a wooden shelf holdin' ammunition. The pot-bellied iron stove was covered in a layer of dust. I wondered if the deputies even thought about the leather whip hangin' on a nail just two feet away from my cell. I had certainly noticed it.

Sheriff Dean took off his hat and slapped it against his thigh as he lumbered across the dry-as-a-bone street to the Eagle's Nest Saloon. He side-stepped some tumbleweeds as they rolled down the street. He stepped onto the wooden sidewalk, looked both ways, then pushed open the batwing doors and stepped inside. He took a moment to let his eyes adjust to the dark, smoky room. He spotted Judge Newman on his regular stool at the end of the wooden plank that served as the bar and walked over.

"Judge, we got a young man at the jail that you need to see."

The ol' judge lifted his head and ran his fingers through his whiskey-soaked, matted gray beard. "Court don't open until Wednesday. Just hold him until then. I got more important matters in front of me." He waved for another shot of firewater.

Sheriff Dean turned on his heels and muttered a curse under his breath. "Why are we stuck with the drunkenest judge in the whole Arizonie Territory?" He nearly knocked the doors off their hinges as he left the saloon and stepped into the street. Out of the corner of his eye he caught a glimpse of a man on a horse. The sheriff used his hat to shield his eyes from the settin' sun.

"Well, I'll be a son of a horse-thievin', no-count, black-hearted whore." He swore just as he felt the bullet from a Colt-Paterson revolver hit him in the chest. No one else saw the blue roan horse as its white-hatted rider slipped into the alley and rode away.

# Chapter Four

"What in tarnation was that?" Deputy Bonney lost his balance and toppled over in his chair.

Deputy Hardin struggled to put his six shooter back in its holster.

I recognized the sound of a Colt revolver from where I stood in the cell. I watched as the two deputies bumped into each other as they tried to fit through the door at the same time. After two tries, they finally extricated themselves from the jail.

"Someone's shot the sheriff! Go git Doc Reid."

I heared someone yell, then I looked at the keys on the desk and pondered, "Should I grab the whip and make a break for it." I knew I could easily escape in the confusion. I heared Loco whinny outside. He was letting me know he was ready. I heared several people shouting and heared more people running toward the scene. I gazed at the keys.

"I might just be better off in here," I thought. "At least that way they cain't accuse me of shootin' the sheriff."

Deputy Bonney rushed back into the jail. "Sheriff's been shot. Looks like he's a goner." He checked to make sure I was still in my cell, then grabbed a shotgun and raced back outside. He ran back in a second later and grabbed a box of shells. I shook my head.

"First the preacher, now the sheriff. Don't seem to be safe for anyone in Rim Rock." I decided to remain where I was for now.

Thirty minutes later both deputies returned. Their

clothes were covered in dirt and Deputy Hardin had the beginnings of a shiner.

"What happened? Is the sheriff gonna make it?"

"Ain't none of your business what happened 'ceptin' the sheriff's dead. You're lucky you's still in here or else you'd be strung up faster than a snake slitherin' through the desert on a hot day."

I looked at Deputy Hardin. He hung up his gun belt and tossed his tin badge on the desk.

"I ain't workin' for you, Bonney. I been h-h-here just as long. I got just as much right to be sheriff as you."

I took a wild stab at what happened between them two sorry excuses for deputies as I watched ex-deputy Hardin stomp out the door. Ten seconds later Mr Lambert, along with two other men, marched into the jail.

"Well, Bonney, what are you gonna do now? If you'da followed my advice, we could have strung up that rascal and the sheriff would still be alive. I say we send a posse out after him again."

It was at this point that he turned his head and noticed me. I waved.

"As you can see, Mr. Lambert, I'm still right here. Ain't no way I could have shot Sheriff Dean. Just like they t'ain't no way I could have shot your preacher t'other day, since I weren't anywhere near here."

He stared at me as if trying to think of a way I could have shot the sheriff from my cell.

"Well, mebbe you didn't shoot Sheriff Dean, but we have an eyewitness who saw you shoot Preacher Tyler."

18

I shrugged my shoulders. I figgered that if'n I wanted to clear my name, I was gonna have to bust out of jail after all. I didn't think Deputy Bonney was smart enough to pour water out of a boot even if he held it upside down, let alone find a coldblooded killer. So far no one had noticed that the leather whip was no longer hangin' on that nail. I glanced at the ring of keys still layin' on the desk. One of the men with Mr. Lambert happened to see them, too. He picked them up, opened a desk drawer and dropped them inside.

"Well, that's shore 'nuff gonna make bustin' out a might more difficult." I thought, as I clenched my jaw.

Two more men ran into the jail. It was gittin' mighty crowded in here.

"Howdy, Mr. Lambert," he tipped his hat. "I just come from the Eagle's Nest. There's five men in there drunker than polecats. They's fixin' to come over here and bust that guy out..." He pointed right at me. "They're gonna stretch his neck pronto."

# Chapter Five

"Well, I ain't gonna try too hard to stop 'em. They might just up and decide to shoot me if'n I try." Deputy Bonney said as he moved toward the window. "Around here a man is guilty until proven innocent. 'Specially a boy who claims to be from Texas."

One of the men from the Eagle's Nest laughed. "I reckon it's kinda hard for a dead man to prove he's innocent. I say we turn him over to the mob."

"You two git back to the ranch and stay outta sight." Mr. Lambert ordered them.

They slipped out the back as Mr. Lambert opened the front door. "Bonney, you and Wesley come with me. Horn, you stay here and keep an eye on that prisoner. I'll see if I can talk to those men."

I stared at the man who had dropped the keys in the drawer. "So you're Clay Horn the famous gunslinger, huh?" I thought as I stared into his eyes.

He chewed on a toothpick with his black hat pulled low over his forehead as his beady black eyes bored a hole right through me. I could see a scar on his right cheek and could smell the wax on his handlebar mustache. Unlike every other gunslinger I had ever heared about, he was dressed in a fine black suit.

"Looks like you ain't gonna git a fair trial," he said.

"Kinda looks that way." I replied anxiously. I wondered if he would just as soon shoot me hisself.

"Yup! Shore's got yoreself in a heep of a mess." He spit out the toothpick and stomped on a scorpion. "I reckon a man's got a right to defend hisself."

"I ain't never kilt no man, Mr. Horn. I just happened to be in the wrong place at the wrongest time."

He glanced over his shoulder at the front door, then back at me.

"Can you hep me out?" I asked without beggin'. If this was my time to die, I wasn't gonna beg like a coward. My late Pa had always taught me to be a man.

He opened the drawer, took out the keys then tossed them at me. "You're gonna have to bust me on my jaw to make it look real. I'll pay you's back for that someday if'n you's live long 'nuff."

"Thanks, Mr. Horn." I opened the cell door and hit him on the jaw before he was ready. He staggered back then fell onto the floor. I whistled for Loco. "Meet me out back!" I hollered, then I scampered out the still open door. I ducked behind a stack of firewood and looked both ways. A few seconds later, Loco trotted up to me.

"Did anyone see you?" I asked as I jumped into the saddle. Loco shook his mane and snorted. "I'll take that as a no. Let's git out of this town. I gotta do some heavy thinkin' and it ain't gonna be in Rim Rock."

As Loco and I jumped over a dry gulch, then sprinted for the brush out back of the jail, I heared a commotion behind me. I heared two bullets whiz by my head. I turned to see Mr. Lambert and Clay Horn. I swear I saw Clay Horn smile as another shot hit the flower of a prickly pear cactus not more'n a foot away. "Loco, he's missin' us on purpose so we can git away. Let's skedaddle!"

# Chapter Six

Four hours later I asked Loco, "I reckon we can keep on headin' toward Californy, or we can stick around here and try to find the man who kilt the sheriff and the preacher. I don't think Mr. Lambert is gonna waste his time lookin' fer us. If you ask me, I think he knows more'n he's lettin' on. I think he might even know who the real killer is."

Loco snorted as he grazed contentedly on the first patch of grass I'd seen since enterin' the Arizonie Territory.

I had a small jackrabbit on a spit. The first meat I'd et in two days. I tore a piece off of the skinny critter as I sat on a boulder with my back up against the rocky slope of the butte. I pondered my sits-e-ation.

"Loco, if they thought I was the man who kilt the preacher cause of you and my hat, then the real killer must have a blue roan horse and a white hat."

Loco pawed the ground and bobbed his head up and down like he understood.

I kinda figgered he did. I remembered hearin' Mr. Lambert orderin' those two men back to the ranch.

"Loco, I reckon we're gonna have to find that ranch. This is what I'm thinkin'. We didn't pass no ranch on the way to Rim Rock and we ain't seen one out west of town. That leaves two directions it could be. I know there ain't nuthin' but desert south of us, so that leaves the north side of town as the only possibility." I was proud of my detectin' ability. "Let's wait till the sun goes down and then make tracks north. I doubt if anyone will be expectin' us to be headin' back toward Rim Rock."

An hour after the sun went down, Loco and I headed out. We traveled slow so to not bump into anyone or anything.

Three hours later we stopped on a ridge that I figgered was about five miles north of Rim Rock.

"Do you reckon that might be the ranch?" I asked Loco.

He raised, then lowered his head as he pawed the dirt.

"Yeah, that's what I think, too. Let's see if'n we can git a bit closer and have a little look-see."

We made our way off of the ridge and I tied Loco to a tree just 'bout a hundred feet from what was prolly the bunkhouse.

"I'll be back soon. I wanna have a look 'round."

He shook his mane, but didn't snort. I knew he was the smartest horse in the whole state of Texas.

I bypassed the bunkhouse after I heared some loud snorin'. I made my way to the barn and opened the door. I grimaced as the rusty hinges squeaked. I waited a minute, but no one stirred. I slipped inside. I counted eight horses, but none of them was a blue roan. I was about to leave when I heared the whinny of one more horse in the other corner. I crept over and saw what could be a blue roan.

"Gotcha!" I whispered, as I lit a match just to be shore. "Now I just gotta learn who you belongs to." I stopped cold as I heared a revolver being cocked.

"I wouldn't do that if'n I was you. Put them hands up as high as you can and turn 'round real slow like."

I did that.

"You're the kid they's lookin' fer in town."

I felt the heat from the match as it burned down.

"I should shoot you right here and save 'em the trouble of stretchin' yore skinny neck."

I saw him take aim just as we both heared a commotion behind him. I yelped as the match burnt my fingers. He fired a shot as I dropped the match.

# Chapter Seven

Loco reared up on his hind legs and kicked him in the back. I heared the bullet hit the wooden beam right beside me.

"Let's make tracks, Loco. Thanks for rescuin' me agin."

We hung 'round just long 'nuff to see a flame in the dry straw. "This barn's gonna burn up faster than a drinkin' man can hide his whiskey from the preacher."

I made shore the horses could escape, then I jumped onto Loco and we high-tailed it out of there. I heared two more shots as the man who owned the blue roan regained his senses. I figgered they wouldn't be able to follow too soon, since all their horses were now runnin' along with me'n Loco.

After two hours of climbin' to a higher elevation, we found an abandoned mine cut into the side of a pine-covered hill. There was just enough room to slip inside out of sight. I took the saddle off of Loco and sat on it as I drank the last drop of water from my canteen.

"I figure we know now who kilt those men, but I doubt anyone will believe me if'n I go back to Rim Rock."

I debated my options. It didn't seem to make a lick of sense to stay any longer in this part of Arizonie. I never met Preacher Tyler and only knew Sheriff Dean 'cause he thought I kilt a man.

"Loco, I still cain't unnerstand why that man kilt the sheriff." I musta sat there for thirty minutes when it dawned on me.

"That's gotta be it! We hasta go back to Rim Rock."

Loco didn't mind when I saddled him up agin. We picked our way carefully down the hill and were soon back in the arid desert. We had to avoid the main trail to Rim Rock and couldn't travel in a straight line 'cause of the gullies. We stopped beside a boulder that was taller than me when I was sittin' in the saddle. I could see the back of the adobe jail from my vantage point a hundred feet away.

"There's only one man I figure we can trust and that's Clay Horn. He might be an outlawin' gunslinger, but he did hep us escape."

I watched a jackrabbit scamper through the mesquite and sagebrush as I listened to my belly growlin'. I didn't have time to think about etin' now. We watched for any sign of Clay Horn for over an hour.

"There he is!" I spotted him outside the low adobe building next to the jail. He was answerin' the call of nature. I whistled like a Great Horned owl to git his attention. He casually finished his business, then looked in my direction. I decided to take a chance he wouldn't shoot me deader than a rustlin' horse thief and stepped out into the open. He looked around and made shore no one was a-lookin', then he slowly ambled in my direction as if he was out for a Sunday stroll. We moved behind the boulder as he held his gun on me.

"What in tarnation are you doin' here, kid? Don'cha know Mr. Lambert has offered a reward for you. Dead or alive!"

"I came back 'cause I know who kilt the preacher

and the sheriff. I mean I don't know his name, but I know he works for Mr. Lambert." I paused for a moment. "Are you gonna shoot me?"

"Naw, I reckon not." He holstered his Colt. "I been workin' for Lambert for two weeks, but I just stay in town. He hired me to keep an eye on his bank. He claims he's a-feared of it bein' robbed. If you ask me, I think he's just makin' shore his loot is safe. I think he's the guy behind a bunch of train robberies and bank holdups."

"I knew he was as crooked as a Bristlecone pine." I stopped yappin' and stared at Clay Horn for a moment. "What would you care 'bout a bunch of robberies. You's just a gunslingin' outlaw."

He drew his gun faster than a streak of lightnin' could knock a man off his feet as we both heared the sound of riders headin' toward town. We watched from alongside the boulder as the men from Lambert's ranch rode into Rim Rock.

"I might as well tell you's the truth," he holstered his gun agin. "I ain't really no outlawin' gunslinger. I been workin' undercover for the Texas Rangers and I tracked Lambert here. That ain't his real name. His real name is Duke Wayne."

I shivered from my boots to the top of my Stetson hat as the name registered in my mind.

# Chapter Eight

"You all right, kid? You look as white as a ghost even though you's covered in dust."

"Did you say that Lambert's real name is Duke Wayne?" I asked as I kicked at the dirt.

"Yeah, why?"

"That lowdown, backstabbin', no-count, son of a scum-suckin' rattlesnake is the man who shot and kilt my Pa. He shot him in the back like a coward! I promised Ma and Clara that if I ever came across him, I would shoot him dead, 'ceptin' I'm gonna shoot him face ta face."

"You even own a gun, kid?"

"Not at the moment, but I know how to shoot a rifle. Pa teached me." I picked up a rock and tossed it as far as I could. "I'm goin' in town and gonna kill that man if'n it's the last thing I do."

"Now hold on thar. You'll git yoreself kilt for shore if'n you just rush into Rim Rock like this. Lambert's men will gun you down as soon as they see ya. We need to think 'bout this and come up with a plan."

We ducked outta sight and spent some time comin' up with a plan.

"I'm gonna head back to town 'cause they still think I'm one of them. You git as close to the back door of the jail as you can. When you see the door open, you make yore way in real quiet like."

I moved up real close to the back of the jail. The door opened and I snuck up real close without bein' seen. Inside the jail I could hear Clay talkin' to Deputy Bonney. I snuck up on Bonney quieter than a mouse in a room full of long-tailed cats. When I was two feet behind him, I pulled out the gun I borreed from Clay. He musta heared summat 'cause he turned his head.

"Remember me?"

"What are you doin'?" Then he looked at the Colt pointed at his chest.

"For right now, we're gonna put you in that cell. If you cooperate and keep nice and quiet, we won't kill ya."

"Horn, ain't you gonna do summat?" He turned his head to the front as Clay aimed his other Colt at him.

"I am gonna do summat, Bonney. I'm gonna stick you in that cell and make you shut up."

He hit Deputy Bonney on the head and knocked him out cold. We drug him into the cell and covered him with a piece of canvas. I put the deputy's hat on and sat in the chair.

"Keep your head down and that hat should fool anyone who wanders in just long 'nuff for you's to pull your gun on 'em. I'm gonna find ol' Judge Newman. He may be a sorry drunk of a judge, but he's an honest one at least. I'll explain everything, then I'm gonna round up Lambert and git him over heres to the jail. We'll stick him in the other cell."

"Are you gonna take him back to Texas?" I asked. I still wanted to shoot him on sight.

"I will if'n I kin, but I won't hesitate to shoot him cold dead if'n I hasta."

Horn turned to walk out the door.

"I don't think you're gonna be doin' any shootin', Horn." Lambert, or Duke Wayne as I now thought of him, stood in the front door holdin' a shotgun.

# Chapter Nine

Clay Horn played it real smart. He couldn't be sure how much Lambert had heared of our conversation. I lay my head on the desk and pretended to be asleep.

"What's goin' on, Mr. Lambert? Why you holdin' that shotgun on me? I was jest headin' over to the bank to stand guard for a time like you wanted."

"Hold on just a dang minute. I heared you sayin' summat to Bonney." Lambert took a step into the jail.

"I was a-tellin' him 'bout this lawman I shot back in New Mexico, but Bonney passed out. There's an empty bottle of firewater on the floor. I reckon you're gonna be havin' to find a new sheriff."

Lambert musta looked at me, saw Bonney's hat and assumed it was him 'cause he swore at me for drinkin' on the job.

"Are you sayin' you want to be the new sheriff, Horn?" Lambert lowered his shotgun.

"Mebbe I am and mebbe I ain't. Why don't we mosey on over to the Eagle's Nest and you and me can discuss it. You'd hafta pay me a lot more money."

They left the jail and I slowly lifted my head. "Phew! That was a close call." I checked the cell to make shore Bonney was still out cold. He was. I jumped up, made shore I had my gun and went to the front door. I peeked around the corner real quick like, then ducked back. Very slowly I took another look. Clay Horn and Duke Wayne were just about to step onto the stairs headin' into the Eagle's Nest. They was a-talkin' but I couldn't hear what they was a-sayin'. Just then I saw an arm emerge around the corner of the building.

"Who in tarnation is that?" I thought, as I saw the barrel of a revolver, then a man. "Whoa Nellie! That's the sidewinder with the blue roan horse and he's a-fixin' to gun down Clay Horn." I knew I didn't have time to call out a warnin', so I's did the next best thing. I let off a shot in the direction of the corner of the saloon.

All at once I heared several shots ring out. One of them hit the doorjamb not two inches away from me. I ducked back inside as I heared the rapid fire of revolvers. After the shootin' stopped, I heared the sound of men trompin' on the wooden sidewalk outside the saloon. I boldly stepped outside fearin' the worst. I was ready to take on the men I assumed had kilt Clay Horn. I was madder than a bunch of hornets fightin' with some wasps over a nest.

The dust cleared, then I saw someone strugglin' to stand up. I was about to plug him when I heared him say.

"Are you all right over there, Rex?"

I recognized Clay Horn's voice. I jumped down off the sidewalk and ran across the dusty street.

"You're alive! I thought for sure they was gonna gun you down."

"They might have done just that if you hadn't fired off that shot when you did. I reckon I owe you my life." He stuck out his hand.

"Aw, shucks, Clay. I didn't do nuthin' special."

Duke Wayne, or Mr. Lambert, as he was known as in Rim Rock, was shot in the shoulder and stomach. He lived just long enough to confess to settin' up the killin' of the preacher. It was all because of the preacher man testifyin' at a trial what sent Duke Wayne's brother to prison.

An hour later, I shook hands with Clay Horn again.

"Well, Rex, my work here is done."

"What are you gonna do now, Clay?" I asked as we mounted our horses.

"I'm goin' home to Abbylene. Are you still gonna head out to Californy?"

I thought about it for a few seconds. "Ya know, I've changed my mind. We never would have known what happened to Pa if he hadn't turned up missing. I think I should go back home and hep out Ma. I kinda miss the place and I even miss Clara, but I'd never tell her that. Would you mind if'n we ride along together?"

It will be good to have the company. Roarin' Plains ain't all that fur from Abbylene."

So we left Rim Rock together. I hoped I would never see it agin. We figgered we'd take our time gittin' back to Texas. A few days later, we reached the top of a ridge.

"It won't be long now. We should be in Abbylene in 'bout two hours."

Just then we heared a rifle shot and Clay's hat flew off. We both dismounted and took cover.

"Who do ya think's shootin' at us now?" I asked as I pulled out my Colt-Paterson.

"T'ain't rightly shore, but I guess we'll soon find out," Clay shouted as the bullets began flyin'.

# HIDING IN PLAINVIEW

## A Rex Ford & Clay Horn Adventure

# Chapter One

"It won't be long now, Rex. We should be in Abbylene in 'bout two hours," Clay Horn mentioned as we paused on top of a ridge. I grabbed my dented canteen and swallered a slug of warm water as my blue roan horse Loco shook his mane and snorted.

Just then we heared a rifle shot and Clay's hat flew away. We both dismounted and took cover behind some white boulders.

"Who do ya think's shootin' at us now?" I pulled out my Colt-Paterson revolver. I used it to smash a scorpion that was a-fixin' to crawl 'cross my boot.

"T'ain't rightly shore, but I guess we'll soon find out," Clay shouted as the bullets began flyin'.

After about thirty seconds we realized that whoever was slingin' lead wasn't comin' close to hittin' their targets. If'n we was indeed the targets. I looked over at Clay and seen that he had reached the same conclusion.

"It must have jest been a lucky shot that got my hat."

I laughed now because it seemed funny. "Good thing you were waving yore hat around to shake out some dust. If'n it had been on yore head, I'd be talkin' to a dead man right 'bout now."

"I reckon that's a shore 'nuff fact, Rex Ford." Clay laughed.

The shootin' stopped, but we stayed where we was for 'bout a minute. Then I heared some whoopin' and hollerin' and two or three horses comin' our way. I stuck my head out from behind the boulder and caught a quick look.

"Clay, it's three Injuns. Should we shoot 'em down, or what?"

He poked his head up jest long 'nuff to see the Injuns. He shook his head and laughed.

"Jest follow my lead," he said.

I didn't know what in tarnation was a-goin' on, but I did what he asked.

When the Injuns was close 'nuff to hit with a throwed rock, Clay stood up and pointed his revolver at the red-skinned savages. I done the same.

"What in the durn state of Texas do you think you're a-doin'?"

The Injuns stopped and one of them held up his hand. He rattled off a whole bunch of talkin', but I didn't unnerstan a word 'xeptin' for "How."

"Cut the Injun talk, Three Feathers," Clay ordered. "I know you speak English jest as good as I do if not even gooder. What do you think yore up to? Shootin' at whatever. You hit my hat. I should plug you right now for that. It was a fairly new hat. I jest got 'er broke in real good."

"My sincerest apologies, Clay. We didn't even see you and your esteemed young companion."

He hopped off'n his horse as easy as hot butter slidin' round in a fryin' pan over a roarin' campfire. The other two savages hopped down, too. One of them walked a ways over to the side, then disappeared outta-site. The biggest one held out a hand. I looked at Clay. He nodded his head.

"Hello, young man. I'm Three Feathers of the Comanche tribe. How may I make reparations? We certainly were unaware of your presence in the area."

I shook his hand. "That's all right. We figgered out that you weren't really shootin' at us." I tilted my head as I looked at Clay.

He laughed. "I reckon you t'ain't never met an Injun like Three Feathers afore."

"To tell you the honest truth, I cain't rightly recall ever meetin' any Injuns afore. I seen some off in the distance when I was in New Mexico Territory."

"Three Feathers is... well, he is..." Clay frowned and pulled on his handlebar mustache as he was a-thinkin'. "You tell him," Clay finally told Three Feathers.

"When I had passed three winters of the frozen white water..."

"Rex here ain't no ijit," Clay insisted, though I had my doubts.

Three Feathers grinned. "When I was three years of age, my father, Running Turtle, sent me to the white man's school in St. Louis."

Clay suddenly crouched down in a shooter's stance and pointed his gun to his left.

## Chapter Two

"Hold it right thar!" Clay shouted.

I drew my revolver as I saw one of the Injuns walkin' toward us. He stopped and held out his hand.

"Lookit, Clay, he's got yore hat." I pointed out.

Clay put his gun away and waved the Injun over. He took his hat and nodded his head. The Injun didn't make a sound, but kinda waved his arm.

"That's Slow Tongue," Three Feathers mentioned. "He hasn't spoken for over a year."

"Cain't he talk?" I asked.

"He's fully capable of speech, but he takes his time about using his words. He is of the opinion we are given a finite number of words to use in this lifetime, and he's saving them for the appropriate time."

I stared at Three Feathers with my mouth open wide 'nuff for a bald eagle to fly in and have 'nuff room to turn round and fly back out.

"My other friend is Jumps Over The Moon, but we call him Jerry for short."

Jerry bowed at the mention of his name. Clay and I both laughed 'cause he were a-wearin' one of them penguin suits.

"I always git a kick out of the names you Injuns give each other." Clay inspected his hat. "I reckon it's got some better ventilation now." Then he plopped it back on his head. "This here's Rex Ford from Roarin' Plains. We's jest gettin' back from Arizonie Territory."

"Were you off on another one of your undercover assignments for the Texas Rangers?"

"Dagnabbitt, Three Feathers. You ain't supposed to know that."

"Sorry, Clay. How may I atone for my lapse of reticence? I didn't mean to betray your identity to Rex."

"T'ain't that. He already knows I'm a Ranger. We jest came from Rim Rock."

"I read in the paper that you eliminated Duke Wayne. Is that correct, or was it simply a ploy to sell newspapers?"

I shook my head at Three Feathers. I didn't unnerstand what all his fancy words meant, and I'm not shore Clay did neither.

"I kilt him if'n that's what yore askin'."

I spoke up. "Duke Wayne was the no-good, scum-suckin', yeller-bellied coward that done shot my Pa in the back. He were usin' the name of Lambert over in Rim Rock. He had a gang of bank robbers and train robbers, but we caught 'em all."

"Excellent! Thank you for making the West a safer place for all mankind."

"Yeah... well... yore welcome, I reckon." I didn't know what to make of Three Feathers. He seemed to be the smartest talkin' man I'd ever come across. White, red or any other color.

Clay told the Injuns, "That's 'nuff of this jawin'. We're gonna head on toward Abbylene and Roarin' Plains. I reckon you's is welcome to foller along with us if'n you want."

"Thank you, but we are headed toward Amarillo. I've been hired to teach at a school there."

"A white man's school?" I asked in jest.

Three Feathers laughed. "Oh, right. I did mention attending a 'white man's school' before. The school in Amarillo is open to students of all ethnicities."

My jaw dropped and my eyes bugged out. "What kind of city did you say?"

"I should have said all kind of people. White, Red or Yellow, as some people refer to Orientals."

I figgered I best keep my trap closed 'cause I was beginnin' to get more confused than ever.

"Well, you jest better quit shootin' off them rifles," Clay warned them.

"I do believe we've used all of our ammunition, so that won't be a problem."

We parted ways with the Injuns. We took our time as we moseyed toward Abbylene. I was a-thinkin' 'bout Ma and my little sister Clara. I reckoned they'd be mighty surprised to see me since the last time I saw 'em, I was leavin' on my way to Californy. I wondered if Clara had gotten married while I were gone. She were fifteen after all. We climbed the last hill 'tween us and Abbylene, when Clay stopped real sudden like.

"What is it?" I squinted my eyes, but I couldn't see nuthin'.

He pointed to a train jest outside of town. "That thar train ain't supposed to be on fire and I can see four riders along side her."

He whipped off his hat faster than a hawk swoopin' down to catch a varmint and swatted his horse. They took off like a bullet from a Henry repeatin' rifle. I reacted as quick as I could.

"Well, Loco," I said. "Here we go again!"

39

# Chapter Three

It took a minute for me'n Loco to ketch up with Clay.

He was hollerin', "C'mon, Horse, faster. Gimme all you's got."

I looked down at his horse. "Ain't yore horse got a name?" I shouted as we raced toward the train faster than a speedin' arrow.

"I reckon his name is Horse. I t'ain't never thought 'bout callin' him summat else."

By the time we pulled up next to the train, we could see that it were the wood car that were on fire. Them other four riders was 'bout a mile away. We could see whar they was headin' so we figgered we best check to see if anyone were hurt on the train. Clay and Horse pulled up next to the engine.

"Rex, you check the ca-boose an see if'n they's anyone hurt back thar."

Me'n Loco trotted carefully along the four cars that made up the train. I kept my eyes peeled and my hand on my revolver as I looked for any sign of activity in them cars. I saw a bunch of people who looked plum sceered out of they's mind. I passed the baggage car and reached the ca-boose.

"Is anyone hurt in thar?"

The brakeman stepped out. "I done been shot in the arm, but it were jest a scratch. Them fellers stopped us from the inside. Two of 'em was a-ridin' on the train. I seen the other two leadin' two extree horses and figgered we was in fer a heap o'trouble."

I hopped down.

"Loco, you stay right here. I'm gonna make shore t'ain't no one hurt on the train."

I could see that the door to the baggage car had been opened as I walked past. I reckoned they had been summat in thar that them durn train robbers had been after. I pulled my gun and took a quick look inside. They weren't nobody in thar. I climbed up on the last passenger car. I took a quick peek inside and didn't see nuthin' 'xeptin' some sceered passengers. I made my way through to the next car and met Clay.

"Everbody is sceered, but they seem to be all right. Two of them no-good bandits was ridin' on the train."

"So that's how they got it stopped. I were a-wonderin' how they done it." Clay shook his head.

"They winged the brakeman, but he's all right. It were jest a scratch."

By now the engineer and the fireman had managed to toss away the burnin' wood. They was ready to head on into Abbylene.

"What are we gonna do, Clay?" We sat on our horses and looked off in the direction the train robbers had gone.

"Well, I reckon it's gonna be up to us to ketch 'em."

We filled our canteens, then started off after them no-good bandits. I could tell Clay had summat on his mind by the way he were fiddlin' with his mustache.

"What is it?"

He spat at a cactus. "I been a-thinkin, that it might not be right for me to 'spect you to do this seein' hows you ain't a Ranger like me."

"I don't mind. Cain't you make me a deputy or a Ranger?"

He thought 'bout it fer a minute as we follered the tracks of them robbers.

"I reckon I can if'n I swear you in." He looked at me. "How old is you?"

I thought 'bout it fer a second. "If'n today is Friday, then I'm eighteen cause this be my birthday."

That seemed to make a difference to Clay.

"All right. Hold up yore right hand."

I did.

"Naw, it's t'other one."

"I held up my other right hand."

Clay thought fer a few seconds.

"Do you swear to... be good to women and children. Take care of widders and orphans?"

"I do."

"Do you swear that you will only shoot and kill outlawin' thieves and robbers and killers?"

"I reckon I wouldn't shoot an innocent man."

"Then by the power of the state of Texas, I, Clay Horn, do make you a Texas Ranger. Now let's ketch them good-fer-nuthin' train robbers."

He slapped his hat against Horse and we took off.

"Didja hear that, Loco? I'm a fer real Texas Ranger now. We gonna ketch us some bad guys."

# Chapter Four

We tracked the train robbers for the better part of two days. We finally traced them to a log cabin on the edge of Plainview, Texas.

"Well, dagnubbit! I'm more surprised than a rooster layin' an egg!" Clay exclaimed. "They've been hidin' in Plainview all this time."

"Whatcha mean, Clay. We jest follered them here."

He twisted his handlebar mustache. "I been investigatin' a series of train robberies for two years. I always suspected it were the same gang."

"What're we gonna do? Should we sneak up on 'em and blast 'em?" I were ready for some real shootin'.

"We're Rangers! We cain't jest bust in and start blazin' away. We need evie-dence." Clay rubbed his jaw.

I couldn't hear nothin' 'xeptin' the sound of two jaybirds squawking over a half-eaten field mouse. "I don't think they's goin' anywhar."

"You could be right. Let's take Loco and Horse over ta the liv'ry and then go over to the saloon and plan out some strategy. I needs me a drink, anyways."

I follered Clay as we snuck over to the main street. I kept lookin' back over my shoulder jest in case the robbers spotted us. We walked into the Wormy Dog Saloon and boy were I knocked off'n my feet. There at a table in plain view were Three Feathers, Slow Tongue and Jumps Over The Moon.

I grinned and spat out my two-day-old toothpick. "Howdy, y'all, or should I say 'how?'"

"Hello there, young Ranger. Have a seat." Three Feathers kicked a chair out fer me.

"It's a pleasure to see you again." Jumps Over The Moon took off his hat and bowed.

Slow Tongue acknowledged my presence with a slight nod. I turned the chair around and sat down.

"Jerry, Slow Tongue and I have been revisiting our plan of going to Amarillo. Jerry thinks it's too far, and Slow Tongue agrees."

I assumed Slow Tongue had merely nodded his agreement, since he weren't too likely to use up any of his precious words.

"What brings you and Clay to Plainview? Did you track the train robbers here. Do you need assistance setting up surveillance?" Three Feathers asked.

Clay stepped to the side as one feller threw another one over the plank that served as the bar and then joined us with a bottle of rotgut whiskey and two glasses. "I'm assumin' you fellers aren't allowed to drink in this fine establishment."

"I do not partake of alcohol in any establishment. Unless it might happen to be twenty-year-old cognac." Three Feathers waved a hand dismissively. "We have decided to stay in Plainview and start an institution of higher education. Assuming I can convince the local women of such a need."

Clay filled our glasses, swallered his at once and refilled his dirty glass. I took a sip and my eyes nearly popped out of my head. My throat burned like a forest fire.

"Do not sip it." Three Feathers suggested. "That

merely prolongs the agony. It is best to follow Clay's example."

"Mebbe I'll jest pass on the whiskey."

"We could use your help if'n you're a-willin'" Clay said.

"Anything to help the cause of justice." Three Feathers pounded the table.

Jumps Over The Moon stood and bowed again.

Slow Tongue nodded.

"This is my plan..."


Later, Clay snuck up on the house where the robbers were hidin'. The Injuns walked down the street pretendin' to be full of the firewater. I were across the way coverin' the front door.

Clay scrambled to the side of the house, flattened hisself against it and snuck a quick peek in the dirt-covered winder. He tilted his head  and then snapped hisself out of sight as someone walked up to the winder. He waited a few seconds and then hightailed it back to the Wormy Dog. I met him there a minute later.

"I gots me a good look at the leader of the train robbers and it's Deen Longley. He's already wanted for robbing five other trains."

"Are we gonna arrest him now?" I asked jest as Three Feathers walked in through the batwing doors.

"I do believe I have misjudged the situation," Three Feathers said jest before one of the train robbers stepped out from behind him with his gun pointed at me'n Clay.

# Chapter Five

I dove to the floor as a bullet shattered the bottle of rotgut. Three Feathers turned quicker than a greased wagon wheel, used his hand as a hatchet and broke the gunman's arm. Jest then another one of the train robbers appeared behind us. *He done snuck in the back door.* I realized.

He let loose with his six-gun. I felt my hair part on the wrong side as a bullet whizzed past. Clay turned in a crouch and with one shot, the feller fell flat on his face deader than a polished brass doorknob. I follered Clay and we turned the dead man over.

"You got him plum smack dab in the middle of his forehead."

"Yeah, but this ain't Deen Longley. He's a-still on the loose.

Three Feathers led the other train robber over to us.

"I do believe I have incapacitated this gentleman, but you might want to toss him in the 'calaboose', as you call the jail."

"Thanks, Three Feathers." Clay nodded as he put his gun away. "Let's let him go and see if he leads us to Longley. I'm shore he has abandoned the house."

Clay and I watched as the injured man staggered slowly down the street holdin' his broke arm with the other one. All at once he took off like a sceered jackrabbit bein' chased by a mountain lion.

"You won't take me alive, Horn!" someone else shouted.

Two shots hit the dirt between me'n Clay. We dove for cover behind the waterin' trough.

"There's three of them and only two of us." I mentioned.

"Sounds like good odds on our part." Clay grinned.

"What're we gonna do?"

Clay poked his head above the trough jest as a horse took a big drink and then snorted.

"Loco! What're you doin'? You's 'posed to be down at the liv'ry."

Loco were just enough cover for Clay to see Longley and the robber with the broke arm sprint into the the land office across from the general store.

"Rex, I want you to cover me from the gen'ral store while I sneak up on them two from the back." Clay looked over at Three Feathers. "You Injuns see if'n you can sneak up on the robbers from the other end of the street."

Three Feathers held a rifle in his hand. "We do not sneak up on white men. Jerry and I will secure the saloon while Slow Tongue reconnoiters the area."

I didn't know what Three Feathers meant, but I nodded and scooted like a crab across the street and into the store. Clay waited until I were inside and then he disappeared like a puff of white smoke inside a barrel of flour. I heared one rifle shot but couldn't tell who shot who. "I hope that weren't you gettin' kilt, Clay," I whispered though no one were around.

A moment later I saw Deen Longley flash across the winder of the land office. I took aim, but he were gone. "I cain't waste any bullets." I checked my supply of ammo. "Dang! I only gots three bullets left."

Clay kicked open the back door of the land office jest as Longley and the other robber flew out the front. He ran to the front door and peeked out real quick. He saw the robber with the broke arm run across the street with a flamin' torch in his hand.

I dropped to the floor as the winder shattered and bullets began slammin' into the barrels of flour and sugar behind me. It were only then that I noticed the back of the store was on fire. "That don't look good!"

Clay took careful aim and fired. The robber with the broke arm didn't have to worry about his arm no more. Longley and the t'other robber scattered like tumbleweeds in the open desert. I looked behind me. "I cain't get out that way." I crawled over a bunch of broken glass to where the front winder used ta be, lifted up and looked out. Two bullets caused me to hit the floor. "Where are you now, Clay?" I heard Loco snort and peeked out the winder again. The street was fillin' up with smoke and I saw three other buildings on fire. I turned around and shook my head. "It's gettin' hotter than a travelin' preacher's sermon in here." The smoke was getting' thicker and thicker. I started coughing up a lung. "I t'ain't gonna let myself be burned up in no store. I got three bullets left, and I'm gonna use 'em."

I scooted out the front door and were jest 'bout to make a run fer it, when I heared someone shout.

"Duck!"

# Chapter Six

I lowered my head and a split-second later the windersill behind me exploded as a bullet struck it. I spun around and saw one of the train robbers takin' aim at me. I figgered I were a goner fer shore, but then I saw Slow Tongue let loose with a knife. Shore 'nuff that knife ended up in the outlaw's chest and he fell over deader than the skunk I done kilt two years ago.

"Thanks!" I shouted to Slow Tongue. He nodded, but didn't say nothing else. I figgered I should feel honored that he used up one of his words on me.

I sprinted down the wooden steps of the general store just in time to see that dirty scum Longley aimin' at Clay. I could barely see through the smoke as I fired my last three bullets as fast as I could squeeze the trigger. Then I stood still as a fence post as I waited for him to shoot me. He swung his gun to the right. I closed my eyes and tried to make myself small. A moment later I heared a thud. I opened my right eye and then my other right eye. The smoke cleared enough, and I saw Deen Longley layin' in the dust.

"That were shore some fine shootin', Rex. I would have shot him myself 'xeptin' I was durn out of bullets. I'm obliged to ya."

"T'weren't nothin'."

Later, after most of the town had burnt to the ground, Clay and I piled up the four dead train robbers on two of their horses.

"Do you reckon there's reward money for ketchin' these outlawin' scum suckin' sons of..."

"There might be, but you's a Ranger now and we don't take reward money for jest doin' our job." Clay informed me.

"Aw, shucks!" I slapped my hat against my thigh to shake out some of the dust. "I were hopin' I'd have me 'nuff money to hep Mom fix up the ranch's leaky roof."

"It is indeed an unfortunate circumstance," Three Feathers said.

"Well, I reckon I can fix up the roof somehow's." I looked at Slow Tongue. "I want to thank you proper for savin' my life." I offered my hand.

He grabbed my wrist in that funny way Injuns have of shakin' hands and nodded. I guess I weren't worth usin' up any more words.

"What are you gonna do now?" Clay asked Three Feathers.

"I am the new administrator of the Plainview education system. I plan to open an institute of higher learning for all qualified students." He waved his arms like he was a-runnin' fer gov'ner. "Of course we will have to rebuild most of the town first."

Clay smiled. "Just don't try to teach anyone how to shoot a rifle."

Jumps Over The Moon hopped along usin' a crooked branch of a Bristlecone Pine for support. I looked down at his foot.

"I have apologized profusely to Jerry for causing the amputation of his toe." Three Feathers helped his friend bow. "I have assured him I was aiming at one of the train robbers."

"Well, I reckon me'n Rex are gonna head to

50

Abbylene with these varmints. Mebbe we'll come back to Plainview someday." Clay untied Horse, put a foot in the stirrup, swung his leg over and settled into the saddle. "Let's ride, Rex!"

Several hours later, Clay and I had jest come out of the Sheriff's office after droppin' off the dead train robbers at the undertakers.

"I appreciate you tellin' the sheriff 'bout how I kilt Deen Longley," I said as I counted out five gold coins.

"Well, now you can be an official Texas Ranger."

Clay and I were walkin' down the street toward the bank when he poked me in the side.

"Wouldja lookee thar! Ain't that the purtiest girl you ever seen?"

I looked over in the direction he were pointin' and couldn't believe my eyes.

"Clara! What are you doin' in Abbylene?"

Just then a man wavin' a revolver with a red bandana over the bottom of his face grabbed my sister around the waist and pulled her into the bank. My feet felt like they was stuck in knee-deep black mud as I heared first a scream, and then two shots.

# THE LAMESA KID STRIKES AGAIN!

## A Rex Ford & Clay Horn Adventure

# Chapter One

"Nobody move a muscle or else I'm gonna plug this lady in the belly," the Lamesa Kid shouted after gettin' everyone's attention with two shots of his revolver. He glanced around the bank and didn't see anyone other than the two tellers 'ceptin' for a mangy dog lyin' next to the pot-bellied stove. "I'll be relievin' you of all the cash and make it snappy."

I looked at my fellow Texas Ranger, Clay Horn, and pulled my Colt-Paterson revolver out of its holster. "I reckon we better get back to work."

"I gots a bad feelin' in my gut about this, Rex. I hates to say it, but I reckon that thar bank robber might be the Lamesa Kid. He's been knowed to be in these parts."

"That ain't the worst of it, Clay. That purty girl you seen was my little sister Clara. That scum-suckin', yeller-bellied-no-good-egg-suckin'-weasel has done taken her hostage."

"I'm a-givin' you jest five seconds to fill this bag with the loot afore I start pluggin' you full of holes," the Lamesa Kid hollered while keepin' his gun pointed at the men. He tossed the bag over the counter and then tied Clara's hands together. "If'n you don't holler, I might jest let you go."

Clara Ford mustered all the courage her fifteen years of surviving on the dusty dry land of Roarin' Plains, Texas, had taught her and nodded. "I won't scream if you promise not to hurt those men."

"We better do what he says," Wilbur Dickens said to his junior teller Dick Micawber.

The tellers stuffed the canvas bag with all the cash it would hold as the Lamesa Kid locked the door and stared out the window. He spotted the two Texas Rangers approaching with guns drawn. He turned back and raced to the teller's cage. "Toss it over and git down on the floor." He waved his gun at Clara. "You're comin' with me, young lassie."

Clara tossed the rope he had used to tie her up at him, folded her arms over her chest, set her jaw, placed her feet firmly in place on the uneven, pine floor and shook her head. "I ain't goin' with you, and I know you don't have the guts to shoot me. You're nuthin' but a manure-smellin' coward who needs a gun to be a man."

The Lamesa Kid picked up his canvas bag and slung it over his left shoulder. He clenched his empty hand into a fist and waved it menacingly at Clara just as he heard voices on the wooden sidewalk in front of the bank. He listened as someone tried to open the door. He fired a shot into the tin ceiling and sprinted for the back door.

Clara waited until she heard the Lamesa Kid mount a horse and ride away. Then she dashed to the front door, unlocked it and threw it open. "The bank's just been robbed!" she shouted startling the town parson and his young wife. "The filthy coward is getting away with all the money."

# Chapter Two

"You go up that side, and I'll sneak up on the far side," Clay said.

"Jest don't go shootin' Clara by mistake," I said tryin' to keep my hand from shakin'.

We got to the bank jest as the parson tried to open the door. We heared a shot and then the sound of boots runnin' along the floor. A few seconds later the door opened and Clay and I took aim.

"Hands in the air," Clay yelled.

The parson and his wife looked whiter than the Indian ghosts I'd seen while campin' out on the desert.

"The bank's been robbed!" Clara shouted again as she stepped onto the sidewalk. She saw Clay pointin' a gun at her and took a step back toward me.

"Clara, is you all right?" I asked while peekin' through the bank winder.

She turned to face me and pointed into the bank. "He ran out the back door." She smiled and stumbled on a loose board.

I holstered my gun and jest had time to catch her in my arms to keep her from fallin'. "What are you doin' here?"

Clay looked inside to make shore it were clear. He seen the two tellers pokin' their heads above the counter and laughed.

"I came to town to get some money for supplies. Ma gave me a list. What are you doin' here? I thought you were headed to Californy."

"I done changed my plans. I'm now a real Texas

Ranger and that's my podner, Clay Horn."

Clay tipped his black hat and said, "Howdy, Miss Clara. I shore hope that varmint didn't scare you too much. Were he the Lamesa Kid?"

"He never gave us his name," Clara said, " and he didn't scare me even when he was pointing that gun at me. I should have brought my rifle with me to town, but I didn't know I'd meet up with a bank robber."

Clay moseyed inside, saw the mangy dog sleepin' in the same spot and checked the back door. He came back a moment later.

"He had a horse tied up back thar. He headed south nears I can tell from the tracks. I reckon we'll have to go after him." He shook his head while rubbing his jaw and straightening his handlebar mustache. "I was hopin' to get a shave and take a hot bath. I t'ain't had one in a month of Sundays. I was fixin' to eat a hot meal and sleep in a real bed tonight. I reckon I'll have to wait till we ketch that durn fool."

"Clara, if'n we bring him back to town, do you think you can identify him as the thief?" I asked tryin' to sound like an experienced lawman.

"I'll never forget that face. He was missin' a piece of his right ear and had a red scar over his right eye. He was missin' two lower teeth and his boots looked like the skin of a rattler."

Clay slapped his dusty hat against his thigh. "That done proves it. She jest described the Lamesa Kid right down to his feet."

I made sure Clara had a room at the Ballou Hotel afore Clay and I took off after the Lamesa Kid. We still had 'nuff daylight to foller his tracks. His horse had a crack in the back right shoe that stood out like a hellfire-and-brimstone preacher in Miss Dorabelle's saloon surrounded by five of her women of the night.

"How far ahead do you reckon he is?" I asked Clay jest as the sun was goin' down.

"The way his horse is limpin' I'd reckon he's only a couple miles or so yonder. He's got to stop fer the night or else he's gonna be walkin' to Mexico."

"Hear that, Loco," I said to my loyal blue roan horse. "We gonna be restin' tonight and roundin' up that stinkin' bandit in the mornin'."

Loco snorted his approval.

Clay patted his horse and laughed. "Hear that, Horse? Loco knows how to unnerstand Ranger talk."

Horse snorted and swished his tail to persuade the horseflies to move along.

"Ain't you ever gonna give yore horse a real name?"

Clay chuckled and shook his head. "T'ain't no reason to do so nows I reckon. We'd both jest git confused."

Clay and I made camp after spottin' a campfire a mile or so ahead ahead jest like Clay reckoned. We made some beans and coffee and watered and fed the horses. We told yarns until we both got too sleepy to keep our eyes open. I were jest about dead to the world when I heared the sound of gunfire in the distance.

"What in tarnation was that?" Clay shouted as he jumped up with his gun cocked.

# Chapter Three

We found the reason for the gunfire jest afore sunup the next mornin'. We found one dead horse and an Injun sittin' on a flat rock with a big lump on his head.

"You keep an eye out for trouble while I talk to this Injun," Clay said as he hopped down from Horse.

I took out my gun, stood up in the stirrups and looked round in all directions but I couldn't see nuthin' but cactus, dust and three tumbleweeds racin' each other to New Mexico.

Clay moseyed up to the Injun with his hand on his holster. He stopped and then laughed.

"May I inquire as to the nature of the levity my precarious situation has placed upon me?"

"What is you doin' out here, Three Feathers?" Clay asked while shrugging to get some of the kinks out of his back from sleepin' on the hard ground. "T'ain't you 'posed to be teachin' at the white man's school in Plainview?"

"That is my intention. However, I was scouting a location closer to my ancestral home near San Angelo. I intend to open a second campus."

Clay tilted his head and twisted his mustache as he tried to decipher what Three Feathers meant.

Three Feathers pointed to the dead horse. "That unfortunate animal belonged to the misguided youth you are apparently pursuing. He managed to sneak up behind me and incapacitated me." Three Feathers rubbed the back of his head.

"You t'ain't much of an Injun if'n you let that boy sneak up behind you. I can still smell his presence and it makes a two-month-dead skunk smell like some of that rose water I were plannin' to use for my annual bath."

"He also stole my horse and alighted in that direction late last night."

"If'n I give you some water, do you reckon you can make it back to town?" Clay asked.

Three Feathers waved a hand. "I can find enough water. I am a Comanche."

"Yeah, you better take some of mine. You couldn't find water if'n you was swimmin' in the Pecos River."

Clay and I made shore Three Feathers had 'nuff water and some hard biscuits to last long 'nuff for him to get back to town. Then we headed off after that scum-suckin', yeller-bellied Lamesa Kid.

"Is you gonna see Clara and your ma when we git back from this?" Clay asked.

"I reckon so. I need to help Ma on the ranch until Clara finds a man to marry."

"She shore is mighty purty," Clay said while we follered the tracks left by Three Feathers' horse.

We stopped after a few miles and I took off my dusty white Stetson and scratched my ear. "Did you notice the same thing I done noticed?" I asked Clay.

He took a long drink of water then laughed like I heared that feller do when he won a hundred dollars off'n Barkis Peggotty the famous gambler from New Orleans.

"Do you reckon that horse is smart 'nuff to go in a big ol' circle and head back to town?" Clay asked.

"I don't know about that horse, but I reckon Loco's smart 'nuff to do it."

We turned the horses and headed straight as a buzzard could fly back to Abbylene. We snuck up on Three Feathers and offered to let him share a ride into town.

"I am much obliged for the offer," Three Feathers said. "I did see that unfortunate youth on the horizon not more than thirty minutes ago. He appeared to be kicking the ground, and I could hear him shouting oaths at my trusty steed as he loped back to Abilene."

"How did yore horse know how to head back to Abbylene without that scum-suckin', yeller-bellied bank robber knowin' he was headin' to the hoosegow?"

"He enjoys the hay at the livery stable more than sagebrush and cactus leaves," Three Feathers said.

We took it nice an' easy on the way back since we knowed the Lamesa Kid t'weren't gonna git away agin. We was jest about a mile from town when both Loco and Horse stopped.

"Did you hear summat?" Clay asked.

I stood up in the saddle and cupped a hand to my best hearin' ear. "If'n I had to guess, I'd reckon that sounds like a herd of stampedin' cattle headin' our way."

Clay looked to his right and and we both seen a cloud of dust that hadn't been there a minute earlier.

"Hang on tight," I said to Three Feathers. "We might be in fer a wild ride."

As soon as I kicked Loco into action, Three Feathers fell straight off the back, landed on a rock and hit his head in the same spot the Lamesa Kid had conked him last night. He looked deader than a petrified tree jest as the first of the stampedin' longhorns came into view.

# Chapter Four

"This is gonna be closer than the first shave with a new straight-razor," I said as I whipped Loco around and straight at the chargin' longhorns. I heared them snortin' and could feel the earth poundin' beneath Loco as we raced back toward Three Feathers who had just sat up and was rubbin' the back of his head without seemin' to hear the stampede comin' right up his tail. "Grab hold!" I hollered as loud as I could. I reached out my hand jest as I looked up into the eyes of the leader of the durn longhorns. "Looks like we t'ain't gonna make it, Loco."

Jest then I heared six quick shots from a revolver and the mighty herd turned directions quicker than bacon curls up in a pan full of hot grease. I grabbed Three Feathers' wrist and whipped him up behind me on Loco. "Is you all right?"

"I do believe you have rescued me once more, Rex Ford," he said as he rubbed his head.

Clay and Horse came to a stop right in front of us and he waved his hat and hollered at the herd. We saw six cowboys charging up from the direction the herd had come. We helped get the herd settled and talked to the trail boss and the point rider.

"My name's Lennox Clickett, and I'm much obliged to ya fer heppin' us out."

Clay shook his hand and said, "It t'weren't no big deal. We heared ya comin' in plenty of time."

I shook my head cuz it were a close call.

"I done lost track of what I were 'posed to be doin'," the point rider said.

He looked about the same age as me, and I reckoned this might have been his first time riding point on a cattle drive. "We got out jest in time," I said. "My name's Rex Ford, and I'm a Texas Ranger. We used ta danger."

Three Feathers snickered behind me.

"I shore am sorry fer what happened. My name's Uriah Steerforth."

We shook hands and then Clay, Three Feathers and myself headed to Abbylene.

"I don't know about yous guys, but I've had more than 'nuff excitement for one mornin'," I said and then took a swaller of warm water from my dented canteen.

"Do ya reckon that Lamesa Kid would be foolish 'nuff to head straight back into the same town where he jest robbed the bank?" Clay asked when we got to the livery stable at the edge of town.

I looked 'cross the street at the Abbylene Bank and shook my head. I waited for Three Feathers to git down and then jumped down myself. I smacked my Stetson against my leg tryin' to shed some of the dust. Then I took Loco into the barn an' told ol' man Murdstone to make sure Loco and Horse were fed, brushed and given 'nuff water to recover from the hunt for that durn Lamesa Kid who done sceered Clara half out of her wits.

Clay stood outside the barn and watched as people scurried along the main street and disappeared into different businesses and some of the homes.

I handed Murdstone enough coins fer a couple days and joined Clay. "Anythin' goin' on? It seems mighty empty fer this time of day."

Clay snorted and pulled on his mustache. "That's jest what I were a-thinkin'. I reckon the Lamesa Kid is holed up somewhere's in the middle of town."

I looked down the street at the tallest building in town, the Ballou Hotel, with no more trouble than an eagle spottin' a tasty rabbit in the bottom of the Grand Canyon.

"You don't reckon he's holed up in the hotel, do ya?"

"I was figurin' it would be either the hotel or Miss Dorabelle's saloon. T'ain't no place else I'd wanna hide."

We checked our revolvers to make shore they was fully loaded and decided to split up.

"I'll take the west side and go up to Miss Dorabelle's place. You hustle 'round behind the buildings to the gen'ral store and come down the east side to the hotel." Clay pointed to the water trough behind the hitchin' post in front of the sheriff's office. "You kin cover me from thar and I'll duck inside Miss Dorabelle's jest as easy and slow as if'n I was fixin' to spend some time at the bar sippin' some of her rotgut whiskey."

"How will I know if you find the Lamesa Kid?" I asked.

"I imagine some gunshots might be the signal."

I nodded and sprinted 'cross the street. I ran as fast as I could behind the buildings without makin' any noise or raisin' 'nuff dust to choke a desert rattler and were soon down yonder at t'other end of town. I walked to the front edge of Buckler's General Store and peeked' round the corner while pointin' my gun at the saloon. I didn't see a soul as I began walkin' slowly toward the Sheriff's

Office. I nodded as I done seen Clay walkin' like he was out fer a Sunday stroll with nuthin' on his mind 'ceptin' a glass of rotgut and a game of poker. He got to Miss Dorabelle's place jest as I hunkered down behind the horse trough. I watched two tumbleweeds chasin' each other out of town and heared some cattle. "I hope that t'ain't the same herd that done stampeded earlier and nearly got me an' Three Feathers kilt dead," I whispered to the annoyin' skeeters big' nuff the carry off a small cow that hovered above the horse trough. I heared Clay whistlin' one of those ol' songs from the war 'tween the states as he pushed open the swingin' batwing doors and stepped inside. I watched the squeaky doors swing back and forth fer a couple times an' then got into position to blast away if the Lamesa Kid showed his face. Nuthin' happened fer a time. I wiped away the sweat from my forehead and swatted at the skeeters which only seemed to rile them up even more.

Finally, I seen Clay edging out the doors with his gun drawn. He looked at me, shook his head and waved in the direction of the hotel. "So, that egg-suckin' skunk is holed up at the Ballou. I will fill his belly full of lead if'n he's harmed a hair on Clara's purty head."

Clay crossed the street using the town well fer cover. He started fer the hotel but I waved him back.

"It's my sister in there," I shouted. I didn't care if the Lamesa Kid heared me. I was a-comin' after him.

"I'll cover ya," Clay hollered.

I edged up to the hotel door and took a deep breath.

# Chapter Five

I glanced over my shoulder at Clay one more time. Then I pointed my gun, busted through the doors and got ready to blast the Lamesa Kid.

"Rex! You're back. I've been so worried about you," Clara said holding a rifle in her arms.

I shoved my revolver back into my holster slicker than goose grease, took two steps forward and stared at the figure sitting on one of the wooden chairs. I looked at Clara and she smiled.

"I bet you're wondering why the Lamesa Kid is sitting there with rope around him."

"I didn't 'spect to see him all trussed up like a Christmas turkey. Why is he bleedin' like he's tryin' to fill a milk pail?"

"I had to convince him to surrender with a little tap on the noggin'," she said with a girlish laugh.

"You did this?" I couldn't believe my little sister could have captured the notorious Lamesa Kid.

"Yup! He came in here all puffed up about robbing the bank. He threatened to shoot Mr. Ballou unless he provided a fresh horse."

"Where is everyone? Are you guardin' this stinkin' scumbag all by yoreself?"

Clara tapped the butt of the rifle and said, "Me and Ol' Henry. I borrowed this from Mr. Ballou earlier because we heard from Three Feathers that the Lamesa Kid was heading into town."

"How did Three Feathers warn you?" I asked jest as Three Feathers, Jumps Over the Moon and Slow

Tongue walked into the room from the back alley. I waved at them and said, "I'll be wantin' to talk to all of you Injuns later."

They sat down at one of the tables.

Three Feathers said, "Jumps Over the Moon and I will certainly explain our version of this debacle, but I doubt if Slow Tongue will want to waste any of his words."

I looked at Slow Tongue. He nodded and crossed his arms over his chest.

"Clara, will you tell me what happened?" I asked.

"I walked up behind him when he was waving his gun at poor Mr. Ballou and gently tapped him on the head."

"She's a lyin' through her teeth," the Lamesa Kid shouted as he struggled to break free.

"If'n you don't sit still, yore gonna knock that chair over," I warned him jest as Clay burst through the swingin' doors with his gun drawn ready to plug someone full of hot lead.

"I reckon we got this sits-i-ation under control," I said with a smile. "Well, I reckon Clara done did most of the work seein' as how she hornswaggled this here scumbag all by her lonesome."

Clay put his gun away and walked up to the Lamesa Kid. He grabbed his hat and threw it over the fancy counter and looked at the kid up close.

"This can't be the Lamesa Kid! He t'ain't no older than a youngun."

"I'm old enough to rob banks and shoot anyone who gits in my way," the Lamesa Kid hollered though now he had done given up tryin' to escape from the ropes.

"He was carrying that canvas bag," Clara said while she pointed toward one of the other tables.

I picked up the bag, opened it and shore 'nuff there was all the loot from the bank robbery.

"I'll be usin' this as evidence when we try you for robbin' the Abbylene Bank," I said. "First, we gonna take you to the jail and keep you there until Judge Redford comes back this way. That should be in two weeks. Until then, Sheriff Micah and his dep-a-ties are gonna make shore you stays put behind bars."

"There ain't no jail in all of Texas strong enough to hold me," the Lamesa Kid hollered and then spit on the floor.

"We'll see 'bout that," I said.

"Do you have a real name?" Clara asked as I untied the kid and jerked him to his feet.

The kid mumbled summat I didn't hear, so I's asked him agin.

"My name is Oliver Brownlow and my pa and brothers will be comin' to Abbylene to break me out of jail jest as soon as they hear 'bout this."

I turned to Clay and saw him straighten out both ends of his handlebar mustache. "Do ya think this scum-suckin' varmint is tellin' the truth?"

"I reckon he might be at that," Clay said. "I t'ain't feared of no man, but the Brownlow Gang is wanted for robbin' trains, banks and saloons and shootin' innocent people in the back. We better get ready fer a shootout."

I looked at Clara and she set her jaw like she was ready to take on the world.

## Chapter Six

"I'm warnin' ya. Pa and my brothers will be comin' here to break me out of jail jest as soon as they hear about this," the Lamesa Kid hollered as soon as Sheriff Micah closed the cell door. "They'll shoot anyone who gits in the way. You'll all end up dead."

"Let 'em come! We got plenty of law abidin' citizens in this town to shoot 'em down like varmints if they try anything," Sheriff Micah said with a smile. He walked to his desk, sat down and locked the cell keys in a drawer. He waved at his deputies. "We need to come up with a plan so one of us is always around to keep an eye on this varmint. He claims his kin will be comin' to bust him out of here." He shrugged and said, "Mebbe so. Mebbe not, but we have to be careful."

"Ma! Look who decided not to go to Californy after all," Clara shouted as me 'n her jumped down from our horses back at the ranch jest outside Roarin' Plains.

Ma stepped out the front door, shielded her eyes against the sun, smiled and said, "I'm mighty pleased ta see ya, son. I heared from Mr. McCain that you are a real Texas Ranger, and you ketched that bandit what's been robbin' banks."

I hopped onto the porch and picked Ma up and hugged her like I ain't seen her for years. I set her down, and she pats her gray dress and fusses with the bun in her hair like she's all embarrassed or summat.

"Rex, you needn't make sech a fuss 'bout seein' your ol' ma."

68

Clara told Ma 'bout the Lamesa Kid while I took care of Loco and her horse Butterfly.

"I've got a chicken and taters for dinner," Ma said. "How long are ya fixin' to stay?"

"Jest long 'nuff to git some things done 'round here," I said back. "I'm gonna fix the roof and make shore there's 'nuff firewood for the winter."

I had done spent four days doin' chores at the ranch when me 'n Clara saw two riders approaching at a gallop.

"Clara, you and Ma best git inside. The way these riders are comin' must mean trouble of some sort. They's ridin' like the devil hisself is jest over the hill and comin' hard."

Clara stepped inside, but I seen her rifle pokin' through the winder jest in case. The riders stopped and made sech a cloud of dust I feared I would choke on ten pounds of dirt.

"Rex! You gotta come back to Abbylene with us," Deputy Potts shouted as he jumped down and nearly fell flat on his face. "The Brownlow Gang robbed the train outside Senora, and they's headin' to Abbylene."

Deputy Hubert took a long drink from his canteen and then said, "We got a telegraph, but then those thievin' outlaws musta cut the lines. The town's cut off. Sheriff Micah and Ranger Horn need yore he'p."

"I'll be saddled and ready to go in two minutes, " I said.

Clara stood in the doorway with her rifle and said, "I'm coming with you."

I shook my head. "No you ain't. Yore jest a girl.

We need men who kin shoot a gun."

"I can ride as hard and fast and shoot as straight as any man. I can knock one eye out of a jackrabbit from a hundred yards and let the other one be."

I couldn't convince her to stay home, so I promised Ma to make Clara stay in the hotel and keep lookout for the gang.

We said goodbye to Ma and headed to Abbylene with the deputies. I spotted Clay and Sheriff Micah outside his office. I told Clara to skedaddle over to the Ballou and git on the roof.

She grinned at me and fer once did what I asked. Me 'n Clay kinda organized the menfolk who knew how to shoot varmints and we waited.

"I can see four riders comin' hard," Clara shouted.

We had the jail purty much surrounded. I didn't see no way four men could kill all of us and break the Lamesa Kid out. He kept on hollerin' that's jest what they was fixin' to do.

"Get ready, men," Clay shouted as we heared the horses.

I had my trusty Colt-Paterson in my hand as four empty horses galloped faster than an eagle can fly straight down Main Street and on out of Abbylene.

"What's goin' on?" I asked Clay. "Where are them scumbags?"

Jest then we heared gunshots and saw smoke comin' out of the bank.

# Chapter Seven

The Brownlows are gonna burn down the town," one of the men said. "We have to protect our homes."

I looked 'round and watched everyone skedaddle. I were glad Sheriff Micah had the keys to the cells with him. Even if the Brownlows got inside the jail, there weren't a way to git the Lamesa Kid out of his cell.

"Rex, I reckon it's jest gonna be me'n you."

"Me and my deputies are still here," Sheriff Micah said. "We ain't gonna let nuthin' happen while we's still breathin' air."

I spotted Clara's rifle on the hotel roof and figgered she's be safe if'n she kept her head down.

We was all takin' cover and keepin' our heads on a swivel like a Great Horned Owl. It were purty quiet fer a time, then I heared a gunshot and Deputy Hubert hollered.

"I done been hit in the leg," Hubert yelled but he fired back and nailed one of the brothers.

Clay hollered that he seen one of the brothers in the telegram office. Deputy Potts done a wrong thing jest then. He eased up from behind a water barrel and someone shot him in the head. He fell down deader than the mule deer I kilt one winter so we'd have some vittles.

I cain't rightly remember 'xactly the way it all happened, but the lead was flyin' thicker than flies on a dead steer fer the next couple minutes. I spotted one of the brothers in the alley 'tween the barber shop and the saloon. I got off a shot that knocked him over but not afore he nailed Sheriff Micah.

"Are you gonna make it?" Clay hollered.

"I'll survive, but the rotten son-of-a-biscuit-eater got me in my shootin' arm. Look out!"

I fired but not in time. Deputy Hubert slumped over, and I could see a big red stain spreadin' out on his shirt. I checked my ammo and reloaded. The way the lead was zippin' through the air, I reckoned them stinkin' varmints would run out afore Clay and I did. I looked up at the hotel roof and hoped Clara was makin' ever' bullet count.

"I'm goin' inside the office to grab all the ammo that's left," Sheriff Micah hollered. We covered him as he dashed inside. By now all the winders was busted and ya couldn't take a step without yore boots steppin' on glass.

"There's one on the roof of Miss Dorabelle's," Clara hollered and then moved jest before a bullet bedded itself in the wood afore her.

I saw the scumbag and took aim. I got him right smack dab in the chest. He stood up fer a time but then he toppled over and landed on his back in the dirt.

I heared ol' man Brownlow yellin' fer the Lamesa Kid to git ready cuz he was comin' to bust him out right then.

"I'm ready, Pa. The sheriff don't look too good. Jest shoot them Rangers and come and git me," the Lamesa Kid shouted.

I checked my ammo and saw I was down to my last bullet. I figgered I could wait til the ol' man got close 'nuff and throw my gun at him. I saw him gittin' ready to do summat.

"Clay, is you hit?" I asked cuz I hadn't heared him

fer a time.

"I took one in the arm and that lucky cud-chewin' skunk creased my head. I cain't see nuthin' 'cause the blood keeps runnin' in my eyes, but I'll be all right."

Pa Brownlow musta heared Clay 'cause he stood up and began walkin' 'cross the street headin' straight as a crow fer the jail. He had a gun in each hand and was firin' at both of us. Clara raised up and took a shot, but she missed when he turned to the side and fired at her.

"I'm all out," Clara hollered.

"Keep yore head down!" I yelled.

The two brothers who had been hit earlier now began throwin' up lead faster than a falcon divin' after a field mouse. I had to keep down to avoid gittin' plugged.

"I'm here, son," Pa Brownlow hollered.

I heared him step on the loose board that always creaked and without even lookin' I stuck my Colt-Paterson around and fired my last bullet. I didn't hear nuthin' fer a time. No one fired at all. I thought about Ma and Clara and stuck my head out jest in time to see that scum-suckin', yeller-bellied-no-good-egg-suckin'-varmint turn to face me. He grinned showin' his tobaccy-stained teeth and pointed his gun right at me. I closed my eyes and reckoned I was a goner. But afore he could squeeze the trigger, he fell flat on his face. I waited a time and then opened my eyes.

"Now how in the world did that arrow git stuck in Brownlow's back?" Clay asked. He had a red kerchief tied 'round his forehead and were standin' beside Three Feathers.

# Chapter Eight

"Three Feathers, I reckon I owe you the skin off'n my eyeteeth," I said. I stuck out my hand and Three feathers shook it mighty hard.

"You are most welcome, Rex Ford," Three Feathers said.

He was the smartest Indian I ever did meet.

Me'n Clay checked on Sheriff Micah. He weren't bleedin' near as much now.

"You's gonna make it," I told him. I gave him part of the curtains to help stop the bleedin'. Then me'n Clay checked on the Brownlow brothers.

""They's a deader than fish out in the desert," Clay said, "and they don't smell near as good."

We could hear the Lamesa Kid hollerin' inside his cell. I went inside and tol' him, "You's ain't gittin' outta here's anytime soon. Yore pa and all your scum-suckin' brothers are deader than last winters beef jerky."

That shut him up real fast, but then he stood up and grabbed them iron bars for all he were worth. He made the ugliest face I ever did see and said, "I'm gonna git you if'n it's the last thing I ever does."

The next day me'n Clara got on our horses and headed home. I figgered we'd help Ma on the ranch. Clay hollered as we left town, "I'm gonna see yous soon."

Well, wouldn't you knows it. I were out choppin' some wood fer the ol' pot-bellied stove one afternoon 'bout a week later jest sweatin' so much I started sinkin' in mud when ol' Clay Horn rides up on Horse whoopin' like the Rebels done in the war to save the Confederacy. I hollered back at him and jest then Ma'n Clara come outside. Clay slid to a stop and hopped off'n his horse jest like he were in a rodeo.

"It's a-mighty good to see ya," I said shakin' his hand.

Clay shook my hand then he took off his black hat and said howdy to Ma. He looked at Clara and smiled. I cain't be shore, but I reckon she done kinda smiled back. I wiped my forehead with the back of my hand and jest kinda laughed. I thought it might be nice if'n Clara 'n' Clay started steppin' out.

Ma cooked up a good rabbit stew. She even added two taters and the last carrot we had in the root cellar.

The next afternoon I done seen another rider comin' toward the ranch like the devil hisself wore on his trail.

He pulled up, jumped off'n his horse and said, "Sheriff Micah needs you. The Lamesa Kid done shot his way outta jail. He stole a horse and headed south. He's gonna join up wit' the Rufus Gaiter Bunch."

Now me'n Clay knew that no-good-bunch of half breeds was known fer stealing horses and generally terrorizin' southern Texas and part of Mexico.

"He needs you 'n' Clay to head up a posse to git them varmints."

Me'n Clay looked at each other.

"Ma, I gotta go, but I'll be back as soon as we git rid of that scum-suckin' skunk."

Clay walked over to Clara. He took off his cowboy hat and jest stood thar. I figgered he wanted to kiss her but didn't know if'n I would shoot him or not.

"I will come back soon's I can," he said.

She smiled and nodded.

Me'n Clay loaded our saddlebags got on our horses and follered the deputy back into town. Jest afore I rode over the hill, I halted Loco, turned back and waved. "We'll be mighty hungry when we git back."

# Captured At Last!

## A Rex Ford & Clay Horn Adventure

# Chapter One

Me'n Loco ketched up to Clay Horn and his mighty steed Horse a few minutes after I dun waved to Ma and my little sister Clara Ford. We was leavin' Roarin' Plains, Texas, to join up with three other Texas Rangers in Abbylene. We was huntin' down the Lamesa Kid and the Rufus Gaiter Bunch. They was all no-good-fer-nuthin' scum-suckin' outlaws that weren't worth the dust in my boots.

"Rex, is you gonna tell yore little sister that I's kinda sweet on her?" Clay asked and then took a swig of warm water from his dented canteen. "I unnerstan' if'n you don't want her to go steppin' out with a Ranger."

Me'n Loco kept trotttin' toward Abbylene as I tried to figure out what to say. Clara were fifteen after all, and weren't married yet. Finally, I said, "I reckon if'n Clara's as sweet on you as you appears to be on her, there t'ain't nuthin' I can say to change yore minds."

"I 'preciate that, Rex. If'n me'n you git back to Roarin' Plains after we ketch them yeller-bellied lower-than-a-sidewinder varmints and git them back in jail, I jest might ask her to go walkin' with me."

I figgered Clara would be downright pleased to go courtin' with Clay. I dun seen her smile at him back at the ranch, and I knowed Ma had taken a likin' to him. She fed him two strips of bacon a day.

We made it back to Abbylene and met up with the other Rangers. Sheriff Micah told us how the Lamesa Kid conked one of the deputies on the head and escaped.

"We was lucky no one got kilt," Sheriff Micah said.

"We's gonna ketch him and fetch him back to jail," Clay said. "If'n we can bring him back alive, I reckon we will, but I wouldn't bet my bacon and beans on that happenin.'"

"Accordin' the the re-ward poster, it don't rightly matter none," Sheriff Micah said.

"We'll do our best to bring him back alive," Clay said, "'cause we is Texas Rangers and that's the code we foller."

Me'n Clay and them three other Rangers loaded up on supplies and ambled outta Abbylene. We figgered since the Lamesa Kid had a week long head start, it weren't likely he'd still be hangin' 'round Abbylene. Clay looked at his map of Texas and thought about where he would go if'n he was tryin' to escape.

"What you thinkin'?" I asked.

He pointed at the map. "This here's mighty bad country. If'n the Lamesa Kid has any brains, he'd head straight fer these hills."

The other Rangers nodded without sayin' a word.

"What's it called?" I asked.

"This here's called Leakey Springs and it's a known hideout fer varmints like the Lamesa Kid."

Outta the corner of my right eye I saw them other Rangers whisperin' to each other.

# Chapter Two

We camped outside Leakey Springs four days later. Clay changed into his disguise and looked like an ol' prospector all hunched over. He wore ol' britches and were wearin' a beard that dun covered his whole face. If'n I hadn't seen him put it on, I wouldn't have recognized him. He went into town and one of them other Rangers headed t'other way to do some scoutin'. Clay came back later that evening and changed outta his disguise.

"Is they there?" I asked. "Did anyone recognize you as a Ranger?"

Clay shook his head. "No, no one looked at me sideways, and I learned the Lamesa Kid left three days ago. He shot and kilt the bartender and made off with all the rotgut. He said he was gonna meet up with the Rufus Gaiter Bunch down near Buffalo Lake."

Jest then I seen the other Ranger moseying back into camp.

"Did ya find their trail?" Clay asked.

"I seen tracks headin' towards Buffalo Lake," he answered.

Clay said, "That settles it. We gonna make tracks fer Buffalo Lake."

We broke camp and headed thataway.


We missed the Lamesa Kid by two days at Buffalo Lake.

"We's gittin' closer," I said to Clay. "We jest mighta had 'em if'n we hadn't lost their trail 'cause of that bad luck. Who'da knowed we would git caught in that box canyon them other Rangers swore was a shortcut."

"Right you are," Clay answered. He looked at them other Rangers and his eyes narrowed down like he were thinkin' 'bout summat real hard.

The other Rangers looked at each and two of them shrugged. I coulda swore on a stack of Bibles I seen the other one smile fer jest a second.

We follered the trail to Mineral Flats and was only a day behind.

"Now we's gettin' close 'nuff to smell 'em," I said to Clay. "Mebbe we should split up in case they decide to make a run fer Mexico."

Clay twisted his mustache while he set 'bout thinkin' agin. "I reckon we's gonna have a better chance if'n we's stick together."

We heared the gang was headin' to Fort Jasper 'cause they was a big ol' bank there.

"I reckon they's gonna rob that bank, but then I wonder if'n they's gonna try to cross the Cotulla Desert or head west. That desert is drier than a church meetin' full of preachers and deacons," Clay said.

# Chapter Three

"They rode off thataway," the local sheriff said when we pulled up. "They shot at me and the preacher but only winged us. They stole all the gold and silver and even took every bit of beans and coffee Jewel Kroger had in her general store."

"Thanks fer yore help," Clay said. "We's gonna water the horses and see if'n we can foller theys trail 'til dark." He tipped his black hat to the sheriff and took care of the horses afore we rode on out of Fort Jasper.

"It's a shame we didn't git there in time to keep them varmints from blowin' up the bank with dynermite and stealin' all the gold and silver," I said.

Clay nodded and added, "To rob the bank is expected of no-good, lowlife scumbags like them, but to take all the beans and coffee were jest uncalled fer."

By the time we crossed the Sierra Blanca Mountains and wandered 'round the Cotulla Desert fer two days, we had lost the trail.

"Where do you think they headed?" I asked Clay. I sat straight up on Loco and looked 'round.

Clay sat up on Horse and used his fancy new lookin' glass he had traded fer in Fort Jasper.

"I don't see a sign of man nor mule. There t'ain't a bit of dust in the air."

We made camp fer the night in the shelter of a butte. In the mornin' I made the last of the coffee and we et the last of the bacon and biscuits. We decided to save our beans for tomorrow.

Clay got out his map and we looked at it tryin' to figger out where them varmints was headed next.

Clay tapped a spot and said, "I heared there was a new territorial bank that jest opened up right here in this town."

"What's it called?" I asked.

"Tumbleweed Gulch, an' it's the most lawless town in Texas."

# Chapter Four

We headed slowly south fer two days. We passed through the towns of Sulphur Springs and then Black Mesa. We were able to find some water and rancid flour in Black Mesa but no beans or coffee.

"We's gonna have to be mighty careful about what we et fer a few days," Clay said.

I looked at the other three Rangers and wondered why they never seemed to be as hungry as me'n Clay. And they always appeared to have a few drops of warm water in their canteens. I reckon I shoulda said summat to Clay but I didn't 'cause I figgered it were jest my mind wanderin' 'round from hunger and bein' thirsty all the time.

We got goin' but at an even slower pace to save Loco and Horse from gittin' too worn out. I managed to kill a rattler one day so we had some vittles that night. Finally, after too many days and nights to remember, we got close to the place where the Rio Grande River makes a sharp bend in a deep canyon. The area was known fer being a favorite hideout fer outlaws from both sides of the river. We could hear guns blastin' and people hollerin' in Tumbleweed Gulch. We was that close.

"I knowed that name were familiar," I said. "Ma's brother lives thar. He's a doctor named Dusty Kimball. He used ta be a gunslinger, but he dun took up doctorin'."

"Mebbe I should meet up with him and find out if'n he knows summat."

Clay used his disguise agin and headed down into the town. I used his lookin' glass and drew my gun 'cause

I figgered the town was only a few feet away. I looked away and it were back where it were afore. I shook my head and wondered how the durn thang could do that. I figgered it was some new contraption Three Feathers had invented.

Clay came back jest afore the sun went down behind the mountains.

"I heared that Rufus Gaiter and his bunch of lowdown skunks had a hideout in the hills but no one knowed jest where."

"Did ya find any grub?" I asked.

Clay handed me a biscuit and part of a piece of jerky.

"I et some of the jerky," he said. "I got bad news."

"What?" I asked.

As I were leavin' I seen Clara head into Doc Kimball's house."

We made camp and I thought 'bout Ma and Clara as we lay under the stars. I could hear coyotes singing somewhere in the hills. I thought 'bout Pa and how he used ta take me'n him campin' when I were jest a young 'un. I wondered if'n I'd ever see either of them agin. I could hear my stomach keepin' time with the coyotes as it rumbled loud 'nuff to rattle my spine.

I woke up first and hunted 'round fer summat to eat. I trapped an ol' jackrabbit and found a few berries. I dug up some roots Three Feathers tol' me were good .

I had jest finished makin' the rabbit and roots into a stew when I heared some riders approaching and firin' rifles.

# Chapter Five

Clay woke up with a start and jumped off'n his bedroll. I grabbed my Colt-Paterson and he grabbed his rifle and both guns. The three other Rangers woke up and we all took cover behind some large boulders.

"Who can it be?' I asked Clay.

"Dunno, but they mean business."

Soon we was firin' at them and they was a-firin' back at us. I heared bullets ricochet off the rocks behind me.

"It's shore 'nuff the Rufus Gaiter Bunch," Clay hollered. "I recognize that feller with the red beard and that scar on his cheek."

"How do ya know who it is?" I asked.

""'Cause I'm the one that dun give him the scar in a tavern fight in Checotah City a few years back when I was workin' undercover."

I looked over my shoulder to make sure the horses were all right. We had hobbled them in a small area surrounded by trees and boulders with a small creek fer water. They was safe as long as they kept quiet. No one would know they was even thar.

"I think I winged one of them varmints," I shouted.

"I got one too," Clay said.

Neither one of us noticed the other Rangers were aimin' at the rocks high above our heads.

The firin' stopped and the varmints rode away. We packed up and rode after 'em. Fer the better part of three days we follered their tracks through the desert.

We lost 'em when they crossed the Hondo River near Palacios Wash.

"What do you wanna do now, Clay?" I asked after we wandered 'round fer the better part of four hours.

"I reckon we should head back to Sulphur Springs to git some grub. We cain't ketch them no-good skunks if'n we starves to death," Clay said.

I felt madder than a hornet bein' attacked by black crows in the early spring 'cause we had been so close to ketchin' them yeller-bellied outlaws.

We made it to Sulphur Springs and this time we loaded up 'nuff vittles and ammo and supplies to last fer a month if'n we was careful 'bout how much we et ever night.

Finally, luck showed up on our side. We were ridin' along the top of this ridge when I spotted the dust from riders in the canyon below.

"Clay! Looky down yonder. Do you reckon that dust is from them varmints?"

We got closer and Clay used his lookin' glass agin.

"Shore 'nuff that's them," he said. "We got 'em this time."

We moved ahead of them when the canyon made four bends that took the outlaws near ten minutes to go five hundred feet while we jest had to head straight to the place where the canyon rose up from the gully.

"You take this spot and I'll lead them to ya," Clay said. "With five of us we can surprise them and git the advantage. We got 'em captured at last!"

The other Rangers nodded and hid down in the dry wash. Now we had the whole canyon covered and could surprise the varmints.

"Wait 'til I say to fire," Clay said.

Soon the outlaws were close 'nuff to smell.

'Now!" Clay hollered. We stood up and fired over their heads jest to make 'em stop.

They stopped and Clay hollered fer them to throw down their guns. I were a little surprised they didn't start shootin' at us, but fer some reason they tossed down their weapons. I looked at Clay and he looked at me.

"I didn't think it would be so easy," Clay said as we walked toward the gang of cutthroats.

"Git down off'n them horses and put yore hands on yore heads," Clay ordered.

Rufus Gaiter laughed and said, "I reckon you had better toss them pistolas on the ground."

I heared three clicks behind me'n Clay. We turned 'round and came face to face with the three other Rangers 'cept now they was aimin' their rifles right at me'n Clay.

We figgered they had us dead, so we dun the smart thing and tossed our guns down. They tied us up and took all our grub.

"I'm gonna leave you with 'nuff water to last a day. Mebbe two," The Lamesa Kid said. "I don't want to kill you and waste the bullets." He held up his hand to block the hot sun and said, "I'm gonna let the sun do that job fer me."

Me'n Clay watched them ride away knowin' they had jest made one big mistake. They left Loco and Horse with us.

# The Heart Of A Texas Ranger

## A Rex Ford & Clay Horn Adventure

# Chapter One

"Looks like it's jest you'n me, Rex," Clay said as them three durn Rangers rode off with the Lamesa Kid and the Rufus Gaiter Bunch.

"I figgered they was trouble from the start, but I didn't want to say nuthin' bad about a Ranger."

"I reckon they stole them badges," Clay said. "I t'ain't never seen 'em afore."

I whistled fer Loco and he'n Horse came trottin' along. Clay was close to a sharp rock so he backed up against it and fifteen minutes later we was both free of the ropes.

"Do we go after them agin?" I asked. "Mebbe we should head back to Tumbleweed Gulch and make shore Clara is safe."

"I shore want to see her safe from all the lowlifes in town but Ol' Doc Kimball will protect her," Clay said.

He opened his saddlebag, got out some of the fancy smellin' wax he used on his handlebar mustache and fixed it up real nice and straight.

"Is you makin' yoreself purty jest in case you see Clara?" I asked with a grin.

"Mebbe I am and mebbe I t'ain't. First we's got us a job to do. We is Texas Rangers and we never give up on findin' the bad guys." He pointed to the West. "They are headin' thataway."

"T'ain't that the di-rection to Tumbleweed Gulch?" I asked with a lump in my parched throat.

"It shore 'nuff is," he answered.

# Chapter Two

Fer the next two days we follered the gang as they changed direction ever few miles. We once got close but it were at night and since we were real low on ammo and vital supplies, we couldn't do nuthin'.

"I hate to even say this, but I reckon one of us has ta head into Yoakum Holler. There be a small Ranger station thar and they will be able to give us some supplies."

"Shouldn't we both go?" I asked.

"If'n we both go the gang might git plum away and we'd have to start trackin' them all over agin. One of us hasta go into town."

"I'll go," I said. "You are a better tracker than me. Remember how you once snuck up on Three Feathers, Slow Tongue and Jumps Over The Moon?"

"I remember," Clay said, " but they's is not smart 'nuff to cover their tracks."

We made plans fer me to meet up agin by the Konawa River jest south of the rock formation that looked like an elephant standin' on its back legs.

"How will I recognize it?"

"You jest have to squint yore eyes and tilt yore head like this." He showed me how he meant. "Then look up toward the Yellow Mesa jest afore the sun goes down, and you'll see a formation that looks like an elephant trying to buck up like a wild stallion."

I nodded but were afeered to say I had never heared of no animal called an ele-phant.

I rode into Yoakum Holler and got 'nuff supplies to last a few days. I figgered it would be over then or else we'd has to give up. We both knowed the Lamesa Kid and Rufus Gaiter's gang was headin' into Mexico soon as they robbed the new territorial bank in Tumbleweed Gulch.

I hightailed it outta Yoakum Holler and were within sight of what I figgered must be  Elephant Rock 'cause it looked like nuthin' I ever seen afore. I were close 'nuff to hit it with spit when I heared rifles blastin' at summat.

# Chapter Three

Loco, we'd better ride hard. Clay might jest be needin' some help and we got the ammunition."

Loco snorted and took off. I hung on fer dear life and we rode into camp jest in time. I jumped down and threw a box of ammo toward Clay.

"I dun got one of them, but I were runnin' low and now they's bein' smart 'nuff to spread out and try to surround us."

I saw one of the varmints and fired at him. I missed but Clay didn't. Now there were one less yeller-bellied skunk out there.

"If'n we don't move away from here by night we's sittin' ducks," Clay said.

I looked 'round and pointed to the Painted Hills. "If'n we can make 'em chase us into thar, we could set up an ambush."

I knew the Painted Hills were farther away than it appeared, but I reckoned it were our ownliest chance to git somewhere safe. We was gonna have ta ride hard. The ownliest problem I could figger were the Painted Hills were only a few miles from Tumbleweed Gulch where Clara be visitin' Doc Kimball and his wife. The outlaws were gonna rob the bank the next day.

"We should wait 'til it gets jest dark 'nuff to give us some cover. If'n we's lucky, we can set up high in the hills and then draw theys attention in the morning."

I took off my white cowboy hat and scratched my head. "How do you reckon we do that?"

"Don't rightly know yet, but fer right now we gotta

keep shootin' 'cause they's comin' agin!"

We used up half our ammo, but we managed to even the odds a bit more. I winged two more and Clay clean knocked one off'n his horse no more than twenty feet from us. He lay in the dirt and soon turned the sand red.

"They's retreatin' agin," Clay said. "Now's our chance to head fer the hills."

We jumped on our horses and rode as fast as a hawk divin' after a rabbit in the desert.

"Do ya think they seen us?" I asked Clay.

"Mebbe, but I don't reckon they's gonna do summat until tomorrow. I figger they's gonna try fer the bank 'round noon when the army payroll arrives."

I looked at Clay and said, "You didn't mention no army payroll."

"I musta forgot. I jest learned 'bout it today."

# Chapter Four

"We gotsa do summat to keep them from robbin' that bank and stealin' the payroll," I said.

"I reckon that's right. I don't like the idea of us jest sittin' here waitin' fer them to pick us off. Mebbe we should head into Tumbleweed Gulch to warn them."

"If'n there's an army payoll comin' into town, won't thar be a patrol to protect it?" I asked.

"You'd think so, but most of the army is in Arizonie lookin' fer them Apaches that hides up in the mountains."

"So it's gonna be up to us to protect that thar money," I said.

"And yer sister Clara and Doc Kimball since he be kinfolk."

"I know she likes to see Doc Kimball and his wife, but she shore picked a bad time to come callin'," I said.

We waited 'til the sun were high 'nuff fer the outlaws to see us. Then we headed toward Tumbleweed Gulch.

"Why did we wait so long?' I asked Clay. "Wouldn't it been better to skedaddle during the night? Only a Great Horned Owl coulda seen us then."

"We can draw some of them away from town if' we head fer Mescalero Mountain. If'n we can draw them there, we can save the payroll," Clay said.

I still didn't unnerstand jest how we were gonna do that, but since Clay had more experience as a Texas Ranger, I went along with the plan.

We headed toward the mountain kinda slow and within a few minutes we could see the outlaws comin' after us.

"It's workin' jest like I planned," Clay said.

"They's gittin' mighty close, Clay. Is you shore this is how the plan were 'posed to work?"

"We jest have ta make it to that thar ridge. Then we's gonna have cover and high ground."

We got to the mountain and set up on the edge of the cliff. We had cover in front of us and didn't have to worry 'bout any varmints sneakin' up on us from behind unless they could fly like an eagle up the sheer cliff.

Them outlaws got kinda careless agin and we picked off a few more. We was gettin' purty sure of the plan when I looked across the river and saw a group of Mexican banditos headin' right fer us.

"Clay," I said then pointed.

"Huh! I never figgered on that," he said and fired agin. Another outlaw landed in a cactus field and never got up.

# Chapter Five

There we was. Jest me'n Clay against the last two varmints we had been chasin' pert near all over the state of Texas. The Lamesa Kid and Rufus Gaiter. We hunkered down best we could on the side of Mescalero Mountain close 'nuff to see the Rio Grande with a five hundred foot cliff two feet in front of us and them durn outlaws to our right. I peeked around a boulder and saw the twenty half-breed banditos comin' from the left. They was ridin' wild mustangs and whoopin' and hollerin' loud 'nuff to wake all the dead buffalo and longhorn steer in the whole territory.

"We best keep a low profile," Clay said. "Mebbe if'n we're lucky, them banditos won't know we's here."

I checked my ammo and since I were down to my last two bullets, I agreed. I knew Loco and Horse was prolly hidin' in the gully where we left 'em.

"They's gittin' close," Clay whispered.

I looked up and saw them two ol' buzzards agin.

It were either them buzzards or the twenty wild banditos that dun it, but jest then the Lamesa Kid stood up, made a dash to a boulder closer to the cliff. Then Rufus Gaiter rolled out from behind his boulder and took a wild shot at us. I figgered he missed 'cause I didn't feel nuthin'. I used one of my bullets and fired. I heared a holler and peeked out. I could see that I had got that polecat square in the middle of his forehead and now the blood was drippin' down his ugly face that must have sceered the doctor and his ma when he was born. It was drippin' down the black matted hair of his beard. I heared a shot from the Lamesa Kid and then he screamed. I heared a thud as he slipped over the edge.

"Looks like we finally got them two varmints, and I still gots one bullet left," I turned to say to Clay. Jest then I saw the bloody hole on the front of his shirt up by his right shoulder.

"I think he got me," Clay said. "He dun got me with that wild shot."

Afore I could say you's gonna be all right to Clay, a Western Diamondback rattler flashed at him and took hold of his other right arm. Faster than greased lightnin' on the Kansas plain on a hot humid summer day that durn rattler had dun got Clay's good arm. I kicked the rattler off the edge of the cliff 'cause I didn't wanna use my last bullet and give away our position to them banditos.

I could feel the hot Texas sun beatin' down on my face. I jest knowed I had to do summat to stop the bleedin' or else Clay were a goner. I remembered how Pa once set his rifle in the hot sun and it got so hot that it fired a bullet. I figgered all I could do was set my gun in the sun and let the barrel get hot 'nuff. I did that and when it so hot I could feel the heat meltin' my leather glove, I slapped the barrel right into the bullet hole on Clay's back and then as fast as I could I slapped it to the front. Somehow Clay managed not to scream as we both could smell the burnin' flesh. I used my spit and what dust I could grab to make some mud and I packed that into place.

"Thanks, podner, but I feel like we're gonna run out of luck real soon."

I told him to lie as still as he could. I still had to

take care of that rattler bite. I warmed up my knife as much as I could. Then I made a X in Clay's arm and sucked out the poison as best I could. I tore off a piece of my shirt and wrapped his arm.

"The ownliest chance we got is to lay low until them banditos move on," I said.

Clay nodded and passed out. I leaned him back so he wouldn't fall off the cliff. We were a quiet as a church mouse lookin' up at a red-tailed hawk 'bout to use him as a meal. I waited a few minutes 'til it got kinda quiet and then peeked at the banditos.

"Well, if that ain't the rottenest luck I ever seen," I whispered even though Clay couldn't hear me. Them banditos had startin' makin' camp not forty feet away.

# Chapter Six

I leaned forward toward the cliff. I couldn't see no way down. 'specially carryin' Clay on my back. I looked up at them buzzards agin. I were tempted to shoot them 'til I remembered I only had one bullet left. I had to figger out summat real fast. I sat thar and let the sun beat down on me'n Clay for a while. I went over all my chances in my head. The ownliest chance I figgered we had would be to wait 'til dark and try to sneak past the banditos.

I waited until them banditos had been sleepin' fer a good three hours. It was blacker than the suit on a undertaker since they wasn't no stars out fer some reason. I figgered that might work to my advantage. I waited until all I could hear was them varmints snorin' like a bunch of skeeters buzzin' 'round yore head. I stood up and waited. No one moved. "They don't have a lookout," I whispered to myself. I grabbed Clay and managed to git him on my back. Then I slipped on a loose rock and started to fall back. I reached out to grab summat afore we both fell down the cliff. I figgered we had dun run outta luck when I caught hold of the only scrub bush around. I held on fer dear life 'til I gained my balance. "That were a close 'un," I whispered. Slower than frozen molasses in the dead of winter I started movin."

It were almost daylight when I finally got me'n Clay clear of the banditos. They was still sleepin' and snorin'. I knowed Loco would be close by, so I whistled as quiet as a pin droppin' on a feather pillow. Loco heared me and he'n Horse came walkin' up nice and easy. I managed to git Clay over Horse. Then I climbed on Loco and tol' him to git us to town. Then I fell asleep.

Loco and Horse made it back to Tumbleweed Gulch and stopped in front of ol' Doc Kimball's house. Loco snorted 'nuff to wake me up. I looked 'round, saw where we was and jumped down.

"Looks like you fellers need a bit of fixin' up," Ol' Doc Kimball said.

Jest then Clara came runnin' outta the house. She gave me a hug and I thought she smelled purtier than fresh honey. Then she saw Clay and gasped. I caught her afore she fainted to the ground. I carried her inside while two men carried Clay into Doc's front parlor. They knocked off Mrs. Kimball's Sunday plates and I heared them crash and break into a hundred pieces. Then they set him on the table. Ol' Doc Kimball tore off Clay's shirt and took a gander at the wounds. He saw what I had dun.

"I reckon you just saved his life," he said.

"I seen my pa do that," I answered.

The Doc began fixin' Clay up. He put fresh bandages on him and tol' us it might be a few days afore we'd know if'n Clay was gonna pull through. The ownliest way we knowed he were still alive were the moans he let loose with every thirty minutes. Clara and me stayed right beside Clay fer the rest of the day. He kept on moanin' once in a while so we knowed he were still alive. I made Clara git some rest and watched Clay all night.

Me'n Clara took turns watchin' over Clay fer the next two days. His moans kept gittin' lower and farther apart. Three Feather, Slow Tongue and Jumps Over The Moon stopped by to see Clay.

Three Feathers and Doc Kimball examined Clay's wounds.

"It appears the wounds are healing slowly," Three Feathers said. "I do not see any signs of infection which is good." He pulled out a snakeskin pouch and handed it to Doc Kimball. "This is a new medicine I have made by combining the roots of the Ghost Plant, some Burro's Tail seeds and the juice from a Living Stone. I have had great success among my people using this combination. It prevents infection and speeds the recovery process."

Three Feathers used some water to blend the ingredients into a paste.

Doc Kimball took a look at the poultice and watched as Three Feathers applied it to Clay's wounds.

"Does it work on snakebites?" I asked. "A rattler got him on his other right arm," I said.

Three Feathers used a different medicine for the snakebite. "This works over ninety-five percent of the time according to my study."

I nodded at Three Feathers and thanked him for being the smartest man I ever did know.

Jumps Over The Moon walked in still dressed up in his penguin suit. He nodded at me.

"Good to see you agin, Jerry," I said remembering

what he liked to be called.

He touched Clay's boots and turned around and walked out. Me'n Clara and Ol' Doc Kimball watched him do a fancy Injun dance in the street.

All this time Slow Tongue was standin' agin the wall and movin' his hands and fingers like he was tryin' to talk to us.

Three Feathers watched Slow Tongue then said, "My friend Slow Tongue has developed a method of communicating by making symbols with his hands and fingers."

Slow Tongue made another motion.

"He also uses gestures to indicate certain wishes and emotions," Three Feathers explained. "This way he can save all his spoken words for later in life."

Slow Tongue continued to make his signs for near another minute. Then he smiled and walked away.

"What did all that movin' and gesturin' say?" I asked.

Three Feathers answered, "He said 'Get well.'"


On the third day Ol' Doc Kimball gave a listen to Clay's heart with his fancy doctoring tool.

"I'm afraid we have done all we could, and it might not have been enough. Three Feathers' medicine is workin', but it needed more time."

Clara cried and I nodded.

An hour went by afore we heared a weak moan. Then it were two hours. Doc said it were up to God now, so I took off my hat and said a prayer.

"God, if'n you's listenin' right now, I want you to

know that Clay Horn has been the best podner a Texas Ranger could ever want. I shore am sorry that no-good varmint Rufus Gaiter plugged Clay with a lucky shot. I t'ain't blamin' that rattler none 'cause it don't know no better."

I kept my hat off and felt Clara touch my shoulder. Then she took hold of Clay's hand and sat right up close. I didn't listen as she whispered summat to him. I figgered she were sayin' goodbye.

Doc Kimball used his fancy doctorin' tool agin. He stood up, looked me right in the eyes and said, "Clay Horn had the heart of a Texas Ranger, but I'm afraid he's gone. I ain't heard a moan for the longest time."

Clara closed her eyes and I did too. We was gonna get up and leave when Clara opened her eyes real sudden like.

"What is it?" I asked.

She smiled and said, "He jest squeezed my hand."

Check out these other titles by the author. Visit the website:
kennethleemcgee.com

<u>The Emmy's Story Series</u>

1. We Were 'posed to Get Married
2. One Of The Guys
3. A New Friend
4. Did You Like the Ravioli Tonight?
5. Completely and Forever: A Wedding
6. It's Time To Go!
7. How Difficult Can It Be?
8. Forever... Isabella... Forever
9. The Forgettable Year
10. Turning Thirty
11. Hello, I'm James
12. Remember The Struggle
13. But God! I Write Songs
14. A Lifelong Dream
15. Gideon's Tree
16. New Priorities
17. Christmas Surprise

<u>The Annie Mercer O'Dell Series</u>

1. Roosevelt High
2. North Park College
3. Smoky Mountain Summer

<u>Stand Alone Books</u>

1. Growing Up In Kinmundy Junction
2. Grandpa, Lions and Kitty Cats: A Collection Of Short Stories For Children Of All Ages